FOR BETTER, FOR WORSE

Jennifer Baker

SCHOLASTIC INC.
New York Toronto London Auckland Sydney

ISBN 0-590-46314-4

Copyright © 1993 by Daniel Weiss Associates, Inc., and Jennifer Baker. All rights reserved. Published by Scholastic Inc.

Produced by Daniel Weiss Associates, Inc.
33 West 17th Street, New York, NY 10011

12 11 10 9 8 7 6 5 4 3 2 1   3 4 5 6 7 8/9

Printed in the U.S.A.   01

First Scholastic printing, June 1993

Julie took a deep breath, a huge gulp of air. "I kissed someone else last night."

A sting of hurt flashed in Matt's eyes. There was a beat of silence. "Who?" he asked. The word felt like a punch.

Julie looked away from his pained gaze. "Don't be mad at him, Matt. It's my fault, not—not Nick's." Her voice dropped to a whisper as she said his name.

There was a stunned silence. Then a blast of fury as Matt punched his fist into the headboard of their bed. "My friend Nick." He spat out his words bitterly. "How could you? How could he?"

"Matt, he was trying to comfort me."

"He was certainly trying to do *something*," Matt said harshly.

Julie blinked hard. "Matt, I love *you*." Matt didn't say anything. Julie watched him as he stared up at the ceiling, his jaw tight, his neck muscles clenched. "I'm sorry. I wish it had never happened."

Matt gave an almost imperceptible shake of his head. "This stinks! I'm off in Riverville thinking about the day we got married—promised our love and devotion to each other—and you're here fooling around with one of the only guys I thought I could count on as a friend."

Don't miss the other books
in this romantic series, **First Comes Love:**

To Have and to Hold

In Sickness and in Health

Till Death Do Us Part

One

🐚

Matt held his goblet up to the midnight-blue sky. Julie raised her glass to touch Matt's, the sound echoing across the black water of the town quarry like a delicate bell.

"Happy one-month anniversary, *Mrs.* Miller-Collins," Matt said.

"Happy anniversary to you," Julie answered. She took a sip of the sweet apple cider. "Mmm. Good year, huh?" she joked.

"Vintage," Matt agreed. His laugh came out in a puff of steam as his warm breath hit the chill of the late-fall air. He snuggled closer to Julie under the big quilt they'd brought with them from home, then grazed her cheek with his lips and traced a soft trail to her mouth.

She turned her face slightly to meet him. Her mouth found his, moist and sweet from the

1

cider. They melted into a deep kiss, warming each other against the night. "Mmm," Julie murmured again. "Even better vintage." She kissed him again.

"Happy?" Matt whispered.

Breathing deeply, Julie nodded. "It's so peaceful." The cold air, which stung her nostrils, carried a delicious hint of smoky wood. Nearby, someone had a fire going. The stars, set in an indigo sky, were reflected in the dark quarry water. "Why do I feel as if this is the first time in ages that I've just done nothing?"

Matt laughed softly. "It's been a crazy few months, huh?"

"Really." Julie put down her glass and worked her arms under the blanket, wrapping them tightly around Matt. It was hard to believe that just a couple of months ago she was saying good-bye to him, going off to college in Ohio, and leaving him behind in Philadelphia. Now they were a married couple, waking up together every morning, sharing every night.

And now Julie had just finished her first half semester at Madison College. Midterms in French and human biology, a ten-page paper in women's lit—she felt confident she'd done an excellent job on all of them. As for journalism, she was happy just to have a few days off from being picked on by Professor Copeland. She could only hope he'd find an undiscovered streak of humanity when he graded the essay tests he'd given that week. Otherwise, the whole class might wind up failing.

But she was too content to think about Professor Copeland right then. Matt put his glass down and returned her hug. Just the two of them under their own private, vast night sky. Julie felt relaxed, calm but with all her senses alive. She was aware of the warmth of their bodies under the blanket, the sharp, pungent air numbing the tip of her nose, the soft, rhythmic sound of the water lapping at the edge of the quarry. "I can't think of a better way to spend my vacation." She sighed happily.

"For those of us who are on vacation," Matt reminded her.

Julie felt a little selfish. "Oh, Matt, I'm sorry." She kissed his cheek, cold from the air. "Here I am feeling totally free, and you have to go off and wait tables tomorrow, same as usual."

Julie felt Matt shrug. "The Barn and Grill's not so bad. If you've got to have bosses, Jake and Pat are about as cool as they come. Oh, they said if it's quiet on Thanksgiving, I can leave early and be home in time to have a real holiday with you. We'll have plenty to be thankful about." He ran his fingers through her thick brown hair and kissed the top of her head, letting his lips linger there for a moment. "Just me and you, Jules," he murmured.

"Just me and you," Julie echoed, but a hint of sadness crept into her voice.

Matt pulled back so that he was looking into her deep-brown eyes. His face was barely visible in the starlight. "Okay, you can be honest, Jules. You're bummed about not spending Thanksgiving with your folks, huh?"

"A little." Julie was mildly surprised by her own feelings. "I mean, it's going to be really romantic, just the two of us and all, but it's the first year ever that I won't be having Thanksgiving with my family." She paused. She had an uncomfortable feeling in the pit of her stomach. "Not being invited home really reminds me of how much they disapprove of us"—she sighed —"not that I need reminding."

Matt's arms still held her close. "Jules, don't forget about how that bill for your tuition just happened to get paid mysteriously. Your folks can't be totally down on you if they were willing to take care of that."

"I know, but still . . ."

"Still what?" Matt stroked her hair.

"Well, neither of my parents has said a word about it."

"And neither have you," Matt reminded her. "I don't get why you're so nervous about thanking them."

Julie shrugged. "Well, if I ever had a chance to talk to Mom alone, I *would* bring it up. I keep thinking that somehow she paid it on the sly— the same way she probably sneaked those Thanksgiving recipes into the mail. You notice Dad hasn't written a word since we got married —or even signed his name to Mom's letters. I know he must hate me."

"It's not you he hates. It's me. I'm the villain. I came out here and eloped with his little girl. I guess I can understand his hating me."

"You think it would have been different if we hadn't eloped?" Julie asked. She answered her own question with a shake of her head. "There's no way they would have approved of our getting married at all." She squeezed Matt even tighter, as though just the thought of being without him might cause him to vanish.

"You're right. Your old man never liked me to begin with," Matt said, a note of bitterness in his words.

"It's not really you, Matt. You know that," Julie said.

5

"I know." Matt rested his head on Julie's shoulder. "If your sister and Mark hadn't been drinking at my dad's club, they probably would have been doing it somewhere else."

"Right. But my dad just can't think straight when it comes to Mary Beth. None of us can." Julie pictured Mary Beth drinking at the Fast Lane. Laughing, dancing, her long, dark hair flying as she spun to the music, tilting a beer bottle to her lips. Mary Beth on her last night alive.

The blue-black sky suddenly seemed dangerously dark to Julie, the woods around the quarry rife with strange hoots and calls. The image of her sister dancing gave way to one of the burned skeleton of a car, crushed against a huge oak tree. Julie's parents had never forgiven Matt's father for serving Mary Beth her final, fatal drink.

"I suppose I'm fooling myself, wishing for a real family Thanksgiving," Julie said tightly. "We haven't been one big, happy family since that night. . . ." Her teeth were chattering now. "I can't stand to think how it must be for Tommy, left at home alone with Mom and Dad."

Matt moved his hands up and down her arms in long, fast strokes, warming her with

6

the friction. "Hey, hey," he whispered. "Tommy's a pretty together kid, and he knows you're only a phone call away." Matt moved his hands to her back. "No more sad thoughts, okay? We're supposed to be celebrating." He kneaded her back muscles with sure fingers.

Julie strove to recapture the peace and calm she'd felt only a few moments ago. She took a deep breath and concentrated on the massaging motion of Matt's hands. When she breathed out, she tried to relax all her muscles, to melt into Matt's steady hold.

"Yeah, that's right," he said softly, drawing her into a hug and punctuating his words with gentle kisses all over her face.

"Well, since I'm a phone call away, maybe I *should* call them," Julie said. "Say happy Thanksgiving to my brother—to my parents, too, even if they're mad at me. . . ."

"Sure. Later," Matt agreed, following the curve of her back with his fingertips. "Right now let's think about how *we're* a family."

The tightness in Julie's muscles was giving way under Matt's tender touch. Her giggle skimmed across the surface of the quarry, her tension escaping with it. "We're a family, huh? The two of us?"

Matt laughed, too. "Yeah. You know, it's the

7

first real family Thanksgiving I'll be having in a long time. Since my mom left. I mean, we've always had the big bash at the Fast Lane. It's a blast, but it's not exactly your basic all-American home-cooked turkey dinner."

"Well, I'll see what I can do about that," Julie promised. "Julie Miller's first turkey."

"Julie Miller-Collins," Matt amended. He nuzzled his face into her neck.

"Hey! Your nose is freezing!" Julie laughed. She reached her hand up and rubbed the tip of his nose, following it with a kiss. Her lips moved up to the spot between his deep-set, gray eyes. She kissed his brow and ran her fingers through his thick, dark hair. She moved her mouth down toward his.

Their lips met. Julie pulled her arms back under the quilt, slipping her hands inside Matt's leather jacket. Their kisses grew deeper, longer, as she felt the slight swell of his chest muscles, his shoulders, his arms. All her worries were swallowed up into the night as he trailed light, soft touches down her back, her arms, the lean length of her jean-clad thighs. He worked her shirt out from the waist of her pants, his fingers gliding along her stomach and up. Warmth of bare skin against skin.

They eased themselves down onto the

ground, the quilt wrapped around them like a cocoon for two. Julie felt her breath coming faster as she drank in Matt's kisses. They strained to press closer.

Julie moved her hands over Matt's body, feeling him return her caresses. Her fingers found the button of his jeans, releasing it, and then her own. Under the shelter of the quilt, they helped each other undress.

"I do love you, Julie," Matt whispered in her ear.

"I love you, too," Julie whispered back.

They made love under the stars and held each other afterward without moving, their breathing mingled with the sound of the water lapping at the quarry's edge.

Two

❧

"New York, four hundred miles," Dahlia Sussman read aloud, grinning as she drove past the sign. "Guess there's just no way of avoiding it," she shouted over the loud music blaring out of the tape deck. "Even out here in the boonies, all signs point to my house. Look at it!" Miles and miles of flat, open land and rows of withered, browned stalks, the remains of the fall corn crop. An occasional batch of bare trees. The light, as flat as the land, the sky a cover of thick, gray clouds. "And at the end of the road, Manhattan," Dahlia said, tossing back her long blond hair. "Pretty weird, huh?"

Nicholas Stone laughed. "I think the New York Chamber of Commerce must send someone all around the country sticking those signs in the ground, just to make sure we all know it's the center of the world."

"Center of the universe," Dahlia corrected with a giggle.

"You mean they give the signs to the astronauts when they send them into space?"

"Probably."

Dahlia had mixed emotions about going back to New York City for Thanksgiving break. On one hand, she'd be there for a few days. Partying with her old pals and club-hopping would be a blast, especially after the past few months in Hicksville, Ohio. On the other hand, there were her parents to deal with—or maybe not. That was the problem. If it wasn't for their annual Thanksgiving with Grandfather Sussman, Dahlia would probably never see her parents. They were always flitting off around the world, leaving her a pile of cash and a stocked refrigerator and telling her to have a good time with her friends.

Still, even being ignored by her parents would be better than sticking around Madison. Dahlia needed some time away from there. She was still trying to figure out how such a good beginning had turned so ugly so fast. One month campus life was a big party: a dormful of students, one huge, happy family; late-night gabfests with her roommate, Julie; and so many cute guys that she couldn't possibly concentrate on schoolwork. Who had time, anyway?

But by the second month, she'd been dumped twice—on the same day. Tim Pike, then Andy Farber, back to back, before she could even catch her breath. She, Dahlia Sussman, the one who'd always done the dumping. The next thing she knew, Julie had run off and gotten married. A blink of her eyes, and Dahlia was living alone—not so different from when she had lived in the cold, glass confines of her New York penthouse, her mom and dad flying off to Greece or Aspen or some other destination of the month.

Dahlia pressed her foot down hard on the gas pedal, and the BMW rocketed ahead through the flat, barren landscape. Okay, she'd get over Tim and Andy—they were just a couple of guys. But what about those things her friend Paul Chase had said to her? Paul, an old pal from New York, was also a freshman at Madison. He'd been madly in love with her, practically since kindergarten. He'd always been ready and willing to do anything to help her out. But rather than be there for her when she really needed him, when she was looking for a shoulder to cry on, he'd been furious, saying she only came around when she needed something. Worse, he informed her that half the campus thought she deserved to get dumped, the way she used guys and stole other girls' boyfriends. According to Paul, everybody was fed up with the selfish, spoiled girl from New York. Dahlia couldn't wait to escape the narrow confines of the campus, where there were no secrets.

"Hey, easy on the pedal, Dahlia," Nick alerted her, pointing to the speedometer. The needle was approaching ninety. "I thought you said you weren't so psyched to get back to New York."

"I'm not, but I want to get out of Ohio fast, that's for sure."

"So turn around and let's go west."

"California?"

"That's west," he agreed. "I could just about afford to split the gas with you."

"Don't worry, Nick. I got the plastic. Daddy'll pay."

Nick raised an eyebrow. *Cute,* Dahlia thought. *Definitely cute.* Julie was right about that. Nick's short-cropped, light-brown hair framed a fine-featured face and dazzling green eyes. Dahlia was glad Julie had insisted they drive home together; Nick lived about an hour north of New York City. If she hadn't said yes right away, it was only because Nick never paid much attention to her on campus. But Julie seemed to think the ride home would change that. She was convinced that Nick and Dahlia would become fast friends. Well, if there was more to him than just his good looks, as Julie promised there was, Dahlia was about to find out.

"So, how about it? Are we going to scrap turkey with the family, turn around and head for California?" Dahlia asked, smiling at him. "How about Colorado instead? Or Utah?" she suggested. This game was getting fun.

"Well, as long as we're dreaming, you really want to know what would be the best?" Nick asked. "New Mexico. We'd park the car there and get some horses, and then we'd hit the old Santa Fe Trail for a couple of days."

"Did I just hear you say horses? As in riding?" Nick had spoken the magic word. "Riding's about my favorite thing in the world. But I never rode western. I learned English. I keep my horse up in Westchester County, not far from where you live. Anyway, Clover, my horse, is so beautiful. I can't wait to see her. Except I might wait—if we head out west." Dahlia laughed.

"Yeah, it would be great. I keep hoping one day I'll get back there. The Southwest is the best. Magical, really," Nick said, a note of yearning in his voice. "Ever been there?"

Dahlia shook her head. "Nope. We were supposed go there last winter to ski Taos, but at the last minute Daddy changed his mind, and we went to the Swiss Alps instead. No, it's about the only place I haven't been. But, hey, there's no time like the present. So what do you say, Nick? Road trip?" she asked. "This thing can do one-twenty, and it feels like you're not even moving. Let's see, at that rate we could be there by . . . ?"

Nick was laughing. "The way you drive, we'd probably be there in time for lunch. Actually, I know this great place in Santa Fe for enchiladas. Homemade and super cheap. I mean it's not fancy or anything . . ." he added, sounding as if he wasn't sure she'd like it.

Dahlia felt a little stung. "Actually, it sounds perfect." Eating enchiladas with a cute guy in New Mexico, a world away from her crazy life —she was liking the idea more and more. She gave Nick a sidelong glance. He'd seemed kind of standoffish at the beginning of the ride, but maybe he was warming up. "So, how do you know so much about the Southwest, anyway?"

she asked. "I thought you said you lived in Chappaqua all your life."

"Well, even us lowly East Coast suburbanites get to travel sometimes," Nick said a little defensively. "I was there last summer on an archaeological dig. I spent six weeks with grad students trying to uncover an ancient Navajo ceremonial site. You wouldn't believe the things you find out there. Remnants of the past, the whole history of the West is everywhere around you. You just dig down a little, and there it is. Totally mysterious."

"Sounds cool."

Nick laughed. "Cool? Oh, it's beyond cool. I found a ceremonial peace pipe that they dated around eighteen hundred. And shards of pottery that could be nearly a thousand years old. And the air, and the mountains and canyons and mesas, unbelievable! And the people, too. Native American, Mexican-American, even a few New Yorkers," he teased.

Dahlia smiled. What a great time they could have, galloping across the desert on horseback, watching the sun set over the mountains. The thought of a steamy, midnight Jacuzzi for two in a hotel with a view out the window of a star-filled sky was just too tempting.

They whizzed past a sign for the next exit,

only a mile away. "Wow, I really would love to just call my folks and tell them I'm not coming home for break—"

"But no way, huh?" Nick said.

Dahlia shrugged. "Normally, it wouldn't be a problem at all. They usually don't even know when I'm around. But Thanksgiving's another story. No, unfortunately Thursday means holiday dinner with Mom, Dad, Gram, and Gramp. And it's not your usual turkey with stuffing and cranberry sauce in front of the fireplace. No, we Sussmans 'do' Thanksgiving. Tavern on the Green in Central Park, pheasant under glass, paté de fois gras, sorbet between courses, and vintage Burgundy. And Grandfather Sussman makes corny speeches about how good America has been to him."

"Sussman? Like the department store?" Nick said.

Dahlia felt herself turning as red as her little car. She nodded. "Bingo. You got it. The one and only. It was my grandfather's. Now my father runs it, and I suppose one day it'll all be mine."

"Amazing! My mom and sister shop there all the time. They'd go naked if it weren't for that place. Wow! Grandpa Sussman," Nick said. He paused, then added, "Now it makes sense, I guess."

Dahlia felt herself tense up. It sounded as though there was a note of disapproval in his voice. "What makes sense?" she asked tightly.

There was a heavy beat of silence before Nick spoke. "Nothing," he said. "I just meant your name, and the store . . . I never realized you were one of those Sussmans."

"Yeah . . . so what about it?" Dahlia clutched the leather-covered steering wheel.

"So, nothing. I didn't mean anything. Really."

Dahlia wanted to believe him, but she knew there was definitely something going on in his head. Silently she completed Nick's sentence the way she was afraid he meant it: *It makes sense, the credit card, the fancy car, and all the things people around campus have said about you being a spoiled rich kid from New York. . . .*

They drove for a while through the cloudy, dull morning, listening to a rock-and-roll tape that Scott and Bob, hallmates from the dorm, had made for her. Dahlia listened to the music and eventually relaxed her grip on the steering wheel. *I'm probably just being oversensitive,* she thought.

"Oh, well." Dahlia shrugged. "Maybe we'll do that road trip some other time."

18

"Yeah, it sounded like fun, but I've really got to get home, too. You know, the folks and all. We've got the whole family in Chappaqua for turkey day. Then on Friday I'm heading into New York to work in this soup kitchen. I usually do it on Christmas and Easter, too. I guess it would be pretty rude to all the people at the shelter if I flaked out on them and headed out to New Mexico. I don't think they'd appreciate the postcard, you know? 'Hi, having a blast in Santa Fe. How's life in New York?'"

Soup kitchen? It was getting clearer every minute. Suddenly Dahlia was absolutely sure Nick must think she was a spoiled brat. "Wow, that's a really nice thing to do," she said. Couldn't Nick see that she cared about people, too? "I gave away a whole bunch of old clothes to a shelter in my neighborhood right before I went to college."

But it was as if Nick hadn't even heard her. "Yeah, I'll be in Manhattan for a day, anyway. I guess I'll have to deal with Allison when I'm there, too," he said, obviously lost in thought.

Dahlia sighed. "Allison's your ex, right? Julie mentioned her to me."

"Huh? Yeah, Allison," he said. "Beautiful on the outside, totally selfish on the inside. And now that she's going to school in Manhattan,

19

she's twice as impossible. Too busy to write, too busy to call. When she needs a little attention, she just gets it from whoever is close by. It took me so long to realize who she really was. I guess the big city's the perfect place for someone like Alli—" Nick stopped speaking. He shot Dahlia a guilty look.

Nick's expression said it all. He might have been talking about Allison, but he thought he was describing Dahlia, too. This was the guy Julie thought would make a great boyfriend for her? A guy who judged her without giving her a chance? The more she thought about it, the angrier she felt herself getting.

"The story I heard, Nick, is that you were out of line going for Allison in the first place. Didn't you steal her from your best friend?"

"That's not really any of your business," Nick snapped. "And besides, you don't know anything about it."

"Well, you don't know anything about me, either—even though you're so sure you do." If it weren't for Julie, Dahlia would have pulled right over and dropped Nick on the side of the road.

There followed a long, uncomfortable silence. An invisible wall suddenly separated them, and it seemed that nothing was going to break it down, not for the next three hundred and fifty-plus bleak miles.

After nearly a half hour of painful quiet, Dahlia realized that the tape they had been listening to had long since ended. She hit the eject button, yanked the tape out, and pushed in another. But when she pressed the play button, the tape deck made a loud whir, then it seemed to short-circuit and it stopped. All of a sudden, the horn started blaring on and off, on and off, all on its own. She punched the dashboard, and the horn stopped.

"Darn it!" she shouted. "What else is going to go wrong?"

Then it started snowing.

"Whoa, it really looks just like it does in the movies!"

Marion Green giggled as her friend Gwen Adams stared out her dorm window at her first snowfall. "Maybe you can collect some in a big bag and take it down south to Montgomery for vacation," Marion joked. "Show it to the whole family."

It was weird to imagine an eighteen-year-old never having seen snow, Marion thought. But then again, there was plenty of stuff she herself had yet to see. Lake Erie was as close as Marion had gotten to the ocean, and she could practically count the times she'd been in an elevator.

"I guess it would have turned into water by the time I got home, wouldn't it?" Gwen asked. Marion and Gwen looked at each other and burst into hysterical giggles. "Well, you're the scientist. You know about these things," Gwen said. "Never mind. I think I know the answer to that one."

"Hey, where are the other triplets?" Marion asked, tying her dark hair back into a single braid. "I want to say bye before my folks come to get me." The other triplets meant Sarah Pike and Amanda Watts, Gwen's roommates. They shared the triple at the end of Marion's hall.

"You missed them," Gwen said as she grabbed a few T-shirts from her bed and stuffed them into an already filled suitcase. "But they told me to give you a giant hug from each of them. They said they'd send you a postcard to your box here and to make sure you did the same. They want to get mail from all over the country. There," she said as she managed to zip up her suitcase. "I'm ready."

"That sounds like fun. I'll send you one, too. Native Ohio farm girl milking cow, or something."

"Great." Gwen laughed.

"But I'm going to miss everyone around here." Marion sighed. "Susan, especially. It's going to be so weird waking up without her on the other side of the room."

"Where's she going, anyway?" Gwen asked.

"She's spending Thanksgiving with her relatives in Chicago. I guess Los Angeles would be a bit far to travel for a long weekend."

"Really," Gwen said. "As it is, I'm going to spend about half my vacation on the bus to Alabama. But I can't wait to see my family. I can already taste my mother's sweet potato pie. Mmm."

"Yeah, I love Thanksgiving at home, too. But I'm even going to miss Bob and Scott and all their music blaring through the halls."

"Bet I know who you're *really* going to miss." Gwen's voice was loaded with implication. Marion felt herself blushing. "Come on, fess up. I know someone who's got it bad when I see her. Where's lover boy, anyway?"

Marion wound a strand of her hair nervously around her index finger. She knew she'd die if Fred didn't come to say good-bye. "He said he'd stop by before his bus came. I don't know, maybe he's in Cincinnati already."

"No way," Gwendolyn assured her. "Fred's as crazy about you as you are about him."

"You think?" Marion asked.

"I know it."

"How can you tell if I can't?"

Gwendolyn gave Marion a long look. "Do you mean he still hasn't kissed you yet?" she asked.

Marion shook her head. She knew that everyone on the hall knew the truth about them. It was no use pretending otherwise. "I don't get it. We have the best time when we're together. We can talk for hours. He's really smart and nice. But whenever it's time to say good-bye, he gets all nervous and shy. Like the other night, we were leaving the library, and we were going to take a walk, out in the field behind the dorm, to watch the stars. He said it was a great night for seeing Ursa Major and Ursa Minor."

"Sounds like the perfect setup for a major kiss to me."

"That's what I was hoping, too."

"So?" Gwen asked.

"Well, the next thing you know, Fred remembers how he'd promised his folks he'd call them at eleven. Exactly eleven, he said. The rates go down then, and his dad gets up for work at five thirty, so he's supposed to call at exactly eleven."

"Uh-oh."

"And as he's telling me this, he's looking at his shoes as if brown loafers are the most interesting thing in the whole world."

Marion could see that Gwen was trying to keep herself from laughing. "Don't laugh, Gwen. It's serious."

"Sorry, it's just the way you tell it."

"Don't think I don't know it." Marion sighed. "I'm starting to go crazy waiting."

Gwen sat down on her bed and shook her head. "Sounds like it's time for you to take action. You have to do a little pushing. You know, let him know what you want."

"I don't know." Marion blushed again. "I guess it sounds sort of dumb, but I keep thinking that next time he's going to make the first move. You know, the part in the book where the boy turns to the girl and gazes down at her and then . . . Well, you know."

Gwen laughed. "Maybe. But I'll bet you'll get what you want faster if you take control."

"Yeah, I know. I've got to let Fred know what's what. But it's going to be hard. I guess I'm sort of shy, too. At this rate, I'll be lucky if something happens by the next Ice Age."

There was a knock on the door. "It's open," Gwen called out.

"I heard some voices, so I thought I might—"

"Fred!" Marion felt herself tense up. "Hi. I was just talking to Gwen." She prayed that Fred didn't hear what they'd been saying. Marion looked at Gwen, who snuck a wink at her.

"Hi, Marion. Hi, Gwen," Fred Fryer said. He looked cute as ever with his Cincinnati Reds cap pulled down, practically to his gold-flecked brown eyes, his freckle-faced grin, his curly red hair poking out under the cap. He tugged nervously at the brim. "I—I wanted to stop by before I left for Cincinnati. I—um, wanted to know what you thought about the midterm, Marion. What about the part about the crayfish's digestive system?"

Uh-oh, Marion thought. He was looking at those loafers again.

"Oh, my gosh," Gwendolyn said, slapping her hand against her knee. "I almost forgot about the laundry I threw in. I'd better go get it before someone helps themselves to all my clean clothes. Have a great Thanksgiving, Fred." She shot Marion a look. "I think the Ice

Age is here," she said as she breezed out of the room.

Fred frowned. "What did she mean by that?" he asked.

"Oh, um, Gwen's never seen snow before," Marion said. She hoped her face wasn't turning a vivid shade of pink. Alone with Fred. She felt a shudder of nervousness race through her. "It's really starting to stick."

"Yeah, I talked to my dad last night. He said they're predicting at least eight or nine inches. Maybe more. You know how they predict the amount—"

"Fred . . ." Marion interrupted. She could see the awkwardness in his face. He looked exactly like she was feeling. "I'm—I'm going to miss you, Fred."

He stared down at the floor. His freckled face got three shades closer to pure red. "Me, too," he said. "I mean, I'm going to miss you, not me. A lot."

Marion held out her hand. Fred seemed to quiver a bit, then took hold of it. His hand was warm and slightly damp. Marion felt a tingling sensation starting in her fingers and going up through her arm. Major accomplishment. She smiled. Fred looked up and smiled back.

They stood there awkwardly for a moment,

holding hands, looking into each other's eyes. Then Marion rose up on tiptoe and, before she could chicken out, pressed her lips to his. Just for a second, but it felt great. "Happy Thanksgiving, Fred."

Three

🖎

"It's going to be weird without you," Tommy was saying, his voice coming through the phone line. "I mean, who am I going to fight with over who gets the drumsticks?"

"Well, you could always snag one for your big sister and wrap it up and send it to me," Julie said, stretching the telephone cord so she was looking out her living-room windows onto the snow-covered Madison Green as she talked.

"Eew, you're still totally gross, Jules." Tommy laughed. "Can you imagine how it'd be after that package went all the way from Philadelphia to Ohio?"

"And sat in my box in the mailroom once it arrived?" Julie added. "Talk about stink bombs!"

"Julie, gross! How am I supposed to look at

that turkey when Dad brings it out tomorrow and starts carving it up? I'm going to be sitting there cracking up."

Julie smiled. "Well, think of me when you do, bro."

"Definitely," Tommy said. "Hey, Jules?"

"Hey, Tommy?"

"Thanks for calling," he said more soberly. "Tell Matt I hope you guys have a great Thanksgiving."

"Sure, Tommy," Julie said. There was a pause.

"So . . ." Tommy said. "You want to talk to—" He lowered his voice. "Dum-de-dum-dum," he intoned.

Julie laughed. She wished she could give her twelve-year-old brother a huge, embarrassing hug right that second. "Yeah, I do want to talk to them—I guess," she said.

"Okay. Happy Thanksgiving, Julie. I miss you. I miss you guys." A plaintive note crept into Tommy's voice.

Julie felt herself choke up. "Us, too, Tommy. We both miss you tons. Keep those letters coming. We want to hear all about Thanksgiving, okay?"

" 'Kay," Tommy agreed.

Julie heard her brother calling downstairs to

her parents. She paced back and forth in front of the windows. With most of the college students gone for the holiday, the Green, blanketed by a thick layer of fresh snow, was unusually quiet. Only an elderly couple, bundled up in overcoats and scarves, strolled down one of the brick walkways that crossed the snow-covered lawn.

Julie felt herself tense up as her mother's voice came over the line. "Julie?" And then, her voice muffled by her hand over the mouthpiece, "Tom, Julie's on the phone. Why don't you take it up in our room?" She returned to Julie. "Hi, honey," she said, a bit guardedly.

It had been this way ever since Julie had called to tell her parents the big news about her and Matt. Now they seemed to expect a bomb to drop every time she phoned home.

"Hi, Mom!" Julie said as brightly as she could. "I just called to wish you a happy Thanksgiving."

"Oh, gee. That's awfully sweet," her mother said, her formal manner giving way a little. Julie could tell that she appreciated her effort. "Happy Thanksgiving to you, too, dear." There was a slight pause. "Did you—did you get my little gift?"

31

The tuition! Julie felt a rush of relief to hear her mother mention it. *"Little?"* She laughed.

"Little what?" her father said sternly, picking up the other extension.

"Oh, hi, Dad," Julie said.

"Just a little something I sent Julie," her mother explained. She sounded flustered. "Some—recipes. Oh, Julie! Did you know that I've been offered a new job as the social worker at the Y? The one you kids used to go to."

"Wow, Mom. That's great!" Julie said, but her mind was still on her tuition. Her mother had snuffed out that conversation as if it were an oven fire. She obviously didn't want Julie's dad to know what she'd done. Julie felt a rush of confused emotion. She was grateful to her mother for her help and generosity, but her father was a different story. Was he going to stay mad at her and Matt forever?

Julie sank into their oversize armchair, one of numerous gifts from Dahlia, who'd found this one at some flea market a few towns away. Her mother talked about her new job, planning the Christmas party they gave every year for her father's congregation, and the new family down the block. Her father said very little. After a few awkward silences, they all wished each other a happy holiday again.

"I hope we'll be celebrating it together again, soon," her mother said.

Her father cleared his throat. "Good-bye, Julie," he said firmly.

Julie swallowed hard. She wished she could tell them she loved them, but the disapproval she felt from them held her back. A cold, silent disapproval, like the cold, silent grief they'd created around Mary Beth's death. "Bye," she said quietly. She put the receiver into its cradle and stared at it. How could they ever celebrate anything together again if her parents couldn't open up? Especially her dad. Open up and accept Matt. She wandered into the kitchen and watched him pouring milk into a bowl of cereal. He turned and smiled at her.

"So? How're my in-laws, the Reverend and Mrs. Miller? How'd it go?"

"Okay, I guess. No huge fight or anything. But they didn't exactly tell me to send their love to you."

Matt carried his cereal over to their dining room table—a big, old door they'd sanded and varnished and balanced on two sawhorses. "I don't expect anything else from your folks," he said, sitting down. "I just feel lousy about what it's doing to you and them." He ate a few bites of cereal, then looked up at her with a sad expression. "Makes me worry that maybe sometimes you wish we hadn't done this."

Julie sat down at the table. She thought about all her friends on their way home to be with their families. Dahlia and Nick were probably halfway to New York by now—and more than halfway to getting together, she hoped. Marion would be in her barn, saying hello to the cows and pigs and goats. Everyone on Julie's old hall would soon be seeing their families. Julie felt a touch of envy.

It wasn't a new sensation. When school was in session, she felt more than a touch of envy. When she was doing extra shifts serving at the dining hall, struggling to help pay the bills, and trying to keep up with her schoolwork, her friends seemed to be having one dorm party after another, going to football games, and trading talk about new CDs. A sigh escaped Julie's lips.

"You *are* sorry," Matt said. He put his spoon down in his bowl.

She looked into his gray eyes and remembered their anniversary celebration at the quarry the night before. Making love under the stars on a cold fall night—who else but Matt could have gotten her out there? The whole night was so romantic. She thought, too, of

their race to Maryland on the back of Matt's motorcycle to get married—another pure adventure. The kind of adventure that Matt lived for. No, Julie wasn't sorry to share it with him. She leaned across the table and gave him a tender kiss. "I don't think I'd have been surprised if someone had told me we'd be getting married one day."

"One day. But not this soon, huh?" Matt asked with a little laugh.

"No, not this soon," Julie agreed. She'd had no idea how lonely it would be at college, surrounded by dormmates and classmates and friends, but without Matt to read out loud to when she came across a really good paragraph in a book, or to giggle with over some comment someone had made in class, or to kiss away a bad day or spirit her off for some spur-of-the-moment fun. The marriage had happened a lot sooner than she'd ever imagined, but she wasn't sorry.

"How about you?" Julie asked, meeting Matt's gaze. "Don't you ever wish you hadn't come out here?"

Matt broke into a grin. "Like when I'm scrubbing pots at the Barn and Grill and waiting on tables at the same time? And when some college jokesters leave a nickel tip on a thirty-dollar tab? Hey, party down," he joked.

"No, I'm serious, Matt. I mean, like when our bills are stacking up and you miss the mountains and the ocean. . . ."

"Sure, I do miss those things. A lot. It's true." Matt nodded slowly, and Julie felt her heart sink. "And it's hard, feeling like I'm on the outside around here. You know, the guy who's not from around here, but not a college student, either. Mr. Nobody."

Julie covered his hand with hers. "Some of us don't think of you that way. I don't. Nick doesn't."

Matt brightened. "Well, I'm not going anywhere, am I?" He turned his palm up and grabbed her hand and squeezed it firmly. "Look, don't pay any attention to my griping. You know I was a basket case in Philadelphia without you." He raised Julie's hand to his lips and kissed each of her fingers. "Besides," he said, "now that all the college Joes have split for break, we're just two regular people living in a regular town, right?"

Julie laughed. "College Joes and *Janes*," she said. "Or Dahlias—or something. Hey, you suppose she's pulled her car over to some scenic overlook yet for a little romantic pit stop?"

Matt shrugged. "She may have, but I really don't think it's going to work, Jules. I don't know why you were so determined to send those guys off together."

"Why not? Dahlia's my best friend here. And Nick's smart and fun—and cute." She drew her hand away from Matt's and frowned. "You just don't like Dahlia. I know you guys got off to a bad start, but she's tried to make up for it."

"By buying us things."

Julie was annoyed. "Things we need. Gifts. And some of the stuff she brought with her from New York. I think that was really nice."

Matt put his hands up in the air. "Okay, okay. I'm sorry. That wasn't very nice. I know. I apologize. I just don't see those two together, okay?"

"Because you think Dahlia's a spoiled brat."

Matt let out a loud breath. "I don't think it really matters what I think. I think it matters what Nick thinks. Julie, the guy's still totally broken up about that girl Allison. You know that."

"Which is why he needs someone else to make him forget about her," Julie said.

Matt frowned. "Julie, why does it matter so much to you?"

37

Julie clicked her tongue. "Because I want my friends to be happy."

Matt pushed his chair away from the table. "How about if you forget about them and we get dressed up really warm and go out and play in the snow?"

"With you? When you're cutting on my friend?" Julie asked, half teasing.

"Jules," Matt said, "Dahlia can be really fun, okay? No, really. I mean it. I just don't think you should get involved in other people's love lives. Now how about it? Snowball fight?" He got up and went over to one of the living room windows. "It's still coming down."

Julie came up behind him and looked out, too. The Green was lost under the powder from the early snowfall. First snow of the year—how could Julie resist? "Well, okay. But get ready. You're going to come out of your snow fort with your hands up, calling uncle."

Matt grinned. "We'll see about that."

Julie grinned, too. It didn't matter what her parents said. Matt was her family now.

Four

❦

Isn't this trip ever going to end? Dahlia wondered. As if the stormy silence that had developed between her and Nick wasn't bad enough, the flakes of snow that had started back around the Ohio-Pennsylvania border had grown into an icy hailstorm, with golf-ball-sized pellets of hail and sleet beating down on the car like a drumroll gone berserk. The early hint of winter had turned into a real blizzard. And, to make matters worse, the little problem with the tape deck and the horn had evolved into a major electrical fiasco. The wipers were barely working, and the heater and defroster were totally shot.

Dahlia shivered as she strained to see a few yards ahead. *Darn, why are you failing me now?*

Just a little longer, baby, she pleaded silently with her car.

"Don't you think we'd better pull over?" Nick asked. It was the first sound of a human voice in over an hour, and there was nothing pleasant about it. Did he think the snowstorm was her fault?

"I'm doing fine," Dahlia snapped. "Besides, we're nowhere near an exit." The truth was, she was nervous. Panicked, to be more precise. There were no other cars on the road, and if they broke down it was going to be a nightmare. But she refused to let Nick see she'd lost her cool.

Nick let out a testy sigh. "Dahlia, how can you even see out the window? Maybe we ought to just pull over and wait till it clears up a little."

"And freeze to death while we wait? If it's all the same with you, I'll take my chances. Besides, isn't your family expecting you?" she asked.

"I never figured I'd be so eager to see them," Nick retorted.

The car crawled slowly through the Pocono Mountains. Dahlia reached up and patted the dashboard. The little engine that could? She could only hope. She had to slow to a snail's pace as the sleety snow got thicker and the visi-

bility even worse. Feeling half blind, she coaxed the car to the next peak in the road.

She couldn't believe that these were the same mountains that had looked so beautiful back in early September when she and Paul had driven out to Madison together. She wished they hadn't had their stupid fight. Then maybe he'd be here now, instead of Nick. At least she'd have a pal along for this horror show of a ride home.

She remembered the landscape lush with green. Driving with the top down, a late-summer breeze blowing, Paul kept shouting and pointing. "Yo! Check out that mountain! Radical! Check out that one!"

Now, Dahlia could barely even see the mountains. And Nick was as far from enthusiastic as was possible. She tried to calculate how much longer they'd have to be in the car together. At the rate they were going, they'd be stuck with each other until turkey time. Even Thanksgiving with stuffy old Grandfather Sussman and her parents would be heaven compared to this.

Suddenly, out of nowhere, the radio started playing, blasting some old big-band song. It sounded to Dahlia like the theme song to "The Flintstones." Then the defroster started to whir, the heater pumped out a gush of glorious warmth, and the wipers arced back and forth at top speed.

Dahlia let out a huge sigh of relief. "All right! I knew this car had a mind of its own!" she cheered, patting the dashboard again like a loving mother. "Like the little engine that could. New York, here I come."

"Weird," Nick said, shaking his head in amazement. "Totally weird."

But just as quickly as everything had started up again, it all shut down in an instant. Dahlia shrieked as a tremendous roar came from somewhere inside the dashboard. It was followed by a series of quick hisses and buzzes, and smoke started billowing out of the heat vents. A noxious smell of burning plastic filled the car. "Oh, my God!" Dahlia screamed. "It's going to blow up!"

Then the wipers, the heat, the radio, everything stopped completely. Somehow, the car was still running. But she could feel it losing power by the second. More and more slowly it went, fighting the strong winds and icy sleet, inching ahead.

"I told you we should have pulled over," Nick said. "The car's shorting out!"

"Like it took a genius to figure that one out. I can't see a thing," she cried.

Nick quickly rolled down the window, leaned out, and reached over to Dahlia's side to wipe away some of the slush. The whipping wind blew a gust of icy snow inside the car, slapping against Dahlia's face and neck.

"What are we going to do?" She clutched the wheel, praying that they'd make it safely, while Nick furiously wiped the windshield clean. What if the car broke down before the next exit? How far was that, anyway? Would anyone come by to help them? Dahlia felt frightened.

"Just keep going," Nick shouted. "Nice and steady, like you're doing." He kept moving the windshield wiper blade back and forth by hand, all the time leaning out of the car.

At least he's good for something, Dahlia thought. She kept driving, Nick's arm marking time like the pendulum of a clock. *Please let there be an exit soon,* Dahlia thought. *Please.* The road stretched out, icy and treacherous. Dahlia felt tears gathering in the corners of her eyes.

Several miles later, Nick pulled himself back into his seat and let out a triumphant cry. "There's a sign up ahead! And an exit ramp!"

Dahlia felt a surge of relief. Food, Gas, Lodging, the sign indicated.

Nick got out of the car and helped Dahlia navigate the sick BMW down the exit ramp and then around an ice-covered rotary. She could make out his waving hands, gesturing for her to turn. Ever so carefully she made her way toward the gas station that was just barely visible in the distance. "Just a little more," he shouted from outside the car. "Careful. Careful!"

Pulling into the tiny, snow-covered gas station felt better than landing on a tropical beach in mid-January. "Finally. Thank God." Dahlia sighed as she shut off the engine. They were stranded in the middle of nowhere, but at least they were alive.

The gap-toothed old man at the gas station, however, was less than thrilled by the prospect of an eleventh-hour repair job before his Thanksgiving vacation. He shook his head at Dahlia and pointed to the sign hanging in the window: CLOSED TILL FRIDAY; HAPPY HOLIDAYS. "Sorry, all locked up," he called to her, his voice riding a whipping wind.

Dahlia got out of the car and ran over to him. "But we have to get home for Thanksgiving. Couldn't you take a quick look at it?"

"Nope," he said flatly.

"I'm sure it's something simple. Please," Dahlia begged. "We have to get to New York."

"Sorry, but I ain't the mechanic. I just pump the gas here."

"But, mister," Dahlia tried again. "We just need the wipers to work. And the heat—"

The man shook his head. " 'Sides, we don't get too many of them foreign cars in here. Nope. Fred'll be in Friday to see what he can do for you. He's the mechanic. It don't look like weather to be driving on the highway, anyhow. It's all gonna freeze up." He nodded toward Nick. "Looks like your friend's frozen already. Better get him in a hot shower. There's a motel right down the road a ways."

A motel? Overnight with Nick? Mr. Mean? No way! Dahlia wasn't about to give up yet. She reached into her car and grabbed her wallet out of her bag. She pulled out all the cash she had. "I'll pay you whatever you like. There must be someone in this lousy town who can fix my car!"

The old man shot Dahlia an angry look. "Lousy town, you say. Maybe so, girlie, but it looks like you're stuck here for the night."

"But, mister—I have to get home."

"And so do I. Family's waiting. I'm telling you, there ain't nobody gonna come out and fix

45

your little car tonight. Not for all that money and then some."

"I'll write you a check, anything!" Dahlia pleaded.

"Dahlia, I think the man is trying to tell you no. Or do you think you can pull out your wallet and fix everything?" Nick's voice was filled with cynicism.

Dahlia ignored his remark. "Well, isn't there a bus? Where's the nearest airport? What about a train?"

"Not till tomorrow." He began walking toward the pickup at the side of the station.

Stuck! It was hopeless. And Dahlia had no one on her side.

The man looked back at them. "You kids plan on standing there all night? Forget about the car, will you? You can leave it right there till Friday. I'll give you a lift to the motel. Hop in."

There was no other choice. Dahlia climbed into the cab of the truck after Nick, and they took off down the road, into the white void.

Five

☙

Matt wove his way through the boisterous crowd at the Barn and Grill, balancing a tray filled with a half-dozen mugs of beer in one hand, high over his head, and a platter of hamburgers and french fries in the other. He'd never seen the place quite like this before. Maybe it was the first snowstorm of the year that had brought everyone, like a bunch of overgrown kids out to play, but more likely it had to do with the fact that all the college students were gone for the holiday weekend. The locals had the town all to themselves, and everyone's spirits were riding high.

"Last call for burgers. Five more minutes and I'm out of here!" Patricia, the cook and co-owner, screamed through the opening between the kitchen and the restaurant.

"Who needs food, anyway?" one of the patrons yelled. "Waiter, more beer! A round of brewskies for me and my buddies."

"Yo, Matt, couple more pitchers over here. There's a party going on," hollered a leather-clad guy at the corner table who seemed to be teetering already.

"Hold your horses, I'm coming," Matt yelled back.

"Yeah, give the kid a break," Jake called out from behind the bar. Jake was in top form that night. The perfect owner for a place like the Barn and Grill, Jake was half college, half townie. He and his wife Pat had both attended Madison and stayed put after graduating. They were as close as Madison students ever got to being thought of as locals.

All the good humor that night was helping Matt feel like part of the place, too. On most nights, when the Barn and Grill was cluttered with students, he felt more like a glorified bus-boy. He'd gotten used to putting himself on automatic pilot as he went around serving, wiping, mopping, doing the dishes, and ringing up the cash register with a humble smile. But that night was different. For the first time, Matt was having fun at work. He felt like his old self. He didn't even feel homesick for the excitement at the Fast Lane; there was plenty of it right here.

"Here you go, ladies." He served the beers and food to a table of six women he thought of as Marcy and the faded jeans gals. All of them were dressed in stone-washed denim from head to toe.

The cowgirl look seemed to go with the decor. Jake and Pat had converted the old barn themselves, leaving lots of touches of the original place: raw wood floors that they had sanded smooth; the hayloft in the back; they had even marked the stables by putting in oak tables where the cows had been penned.

"Thanks, Matt." Marcy slapped a twenty on his tray and patted him on the back. "Keep the change, honey."

Matt smiled. He barely had a second to say thanks before there were three more beer requests, and then somebody spilled a pitcher. The shatter of glass on the hardwood floor only seemed to add to all the excitement.

"Sweet home, Alabama!" Mr. Leather-clad hollered along to the music that poured out of the jukebox. "Gonna move there one day, I swear I will!"

"Why bother?" another drunken voice boomed back over the clatter. "They got college kids down there, too." The whole place exploded with laughter.

Matt couldn't help but do the same. He felt a twinge of guilt, being married to "a college kid," but he understood how the crowd felt. The students came in here fresh from Mom and Dad's house, acting like they owned the town. And they treated Matt and any other working person like a hired hand. Sure, the locals made Matt work his butt off, too, but at least they had a sense of humor about things. And, unlike the college kids, the townies tipped well.

"Hey, Duane," someone yelled across the room, "I think I'm gonna go to college next year."

"And why's that, Billy?" he shouted back.

"Then I won't have to work for the next four years."

"Knowing you, Billy, it'll take you a lot longer than that to graduate from college. Heck, didn't it take you three years to get through seventh grade?" Roars of hysterical laughter swelled all the way up to the hayloft.

Matt cleared plates from a few tables, promising more customers that he'd bring them their beers as soon as he could. Then he hurried into the kitchen to grab a broom and a dustpan for the broken glass.

Pat was taking off her apron. "I'm out of here," she said, wiping the sweat from her brow. She took a couple of bobby pins out of her hair, and a wave of dark blond hair fell down to her shoulders. "Wow! It's really wild out there tonight. You sure you and Jake are going to be okay on your own, Matt?"

"You kidding? They're tame compared to the Fast Lane on a Friday night. It's like this times a hundred in Philly," he said.

"Then your dad must really rake it in, 'cause we're doing a whopping business tonight. Jake and I could retire young if every night was like this."

"Me, too." Matt grinned and patted a pocketful of tips. "Looks like rent money and the phone bill are taken care of. Finally." He sighed.

Pat smiled back at Matt. "You and Julie are going to make out just fine. I know it."

"Thanks, Pat. I sure hope so."

Matt heard another scream for beer. "We're empty. Where's my boy?"

"Sweet music to my ears." Matt hurried back to the crowded room, where he picked up a tray from the bar and got his instructions from Jake.

Jake pointed to a guy and girl who were sharing a single chair, lost to the world in a passionate embrace. "The mugs are for the lovebirds and the pitcher's for Carl and his crew."

Matt placed the mugs on the couple's table and cleared his throat. He caught the eye of the guy, who managed to keep his lips locked tightly against his girlfriend's while at the same time placing a bill in Matt's hand and motioning for him to split.

"Raking it in tonight, huh, Matt?"

Matt turned around. "Hey, buddy. I didn't know you were here. How you doing, Lip?"

"Cool." Leon Davis, "Lip," as he was known, because he played a mean saxophone, was sitting alone at a corner table, surveying the scene. The sensitive-musician type, he was often seen around town by himself, sitting in the coffee shop or outside on the Green with his eyes closed, trying to come up with another jazz riff. "You don't have to play it to hear it," he had told Matt once. Matt had had a chance to hear him play, too. Even before they'd really gotten to know each other, Matt felt a bond with him. Matt loved music, and Lip played it great. He was worthy of his nickname.

"All by yourself, Lip?" Matt asked.

"What are you talking about, man, the place is packed. I'm enjoying the party."

Matt laughed. "Let me get you a beer. On the house, pal. From one pauper to another."

"Cool." Leon smiled back.

"Mug of draft, Jake," Matt called out.

"Yo, you got to stop by my place one of these days and hear some of the new stuff I've been working on. I've got just about enough to cut a disc. Real bebop, like the old days."

"Sounds great," Matt said. "I'm psyched. Let's definitely hang out soon."

Matt wished it could be like this every night. Lots of laughs, lots of smiles, lots of tips. Permanent college vacation. He'd miss Nick, but that was about it.

Matt felt a hand grab hold of his arm as he passed a table. "Oh, sorry, Carl. Here's your pitcher." He took a pitcher from his tray, put it down on the table, and picked up the empty one. But Carl Sever kept hold of Matt's arm. "What's up, Carl?" Matt asked.

He pulled Matt close to his face. "How you doing, man?" he asked, a wide grin on his face.

Like every Friday night, Carl was lit. And

there was more than just beer on his breath. Matt was sure he had snuck in a bottle of Jack Daniel's or something just as strong. "I'm fine, Carl. Busy, though," Matt said politely, trying to pull away.

"How 'bout the missus? Where's your pretty little college girl tonight? She ain't got her friends in town. Must be lonely."

Matt didn't like where this conversation was going at all. "She's home."

"Yeah, she's fine, man. A fine girl. What's her name, Julie?" Carl continued, his voice rising. "Sweet Julie. Sweet, sweet Julie."

"Cool it, Carl," one of his drinking buddies warned him. "Don't mind him," the guy said to Matt. "He's just had one too many tonight. He didn't mean it, man. Tough day at work, you know?" he said, grabbing Carl by the shoulder and yanking him away from Matt.

Matt knew Carl's type well enough. Worked hard, partied harder. He was okay—so long as he wasn't bombed. But every so often, after a couple too many rounds, he'd start to shoot his mouth off. Basically harmless, though. Matt had years of experience with Carl's sort of drunken babble. Still, he didn't need to hear Carl blabbering about his own wife. He tried to keep his anger in check.

"Sweet Julie." Carl's voice started to rise above the others. He didn't seem ready to quiet down yet. He got up and stood on his chair. The noise level in the restaurant dipped as people turned to watch him. "Does sweet Julie have a friend for me, man? Sure she does. A fine, young *college* girl just waiting to meet ole Carl. Huh, Matt? What do you say, buddy? Ole Carl's waiting."

"Shut up, Carl," his friend shouted.

"I said, I want a college girl! Just like everybody else in this joint is dreaming of. Well, I'm gonna get me one, just see if I don't—"

"Shut your mouth!" His friend yanked him down off the chair and pushed him hard in the chest. Carl was teetering. "That's enough. You made a fool enough of yourself already."

Carl seemed to sober up a little. He shrugged his shoulders. "Hey, I was just fooling around, man. Just kidding. What'd you hit me like that for?" he asked, sounding confused.

"Hit him again. Teach him a little something," somebody yelled out.

"What do you say we all settle down?" Jake had come over to the table. "There'll be no fighting at the Barn and Grill. Not tonight, not ever. Now how would you boys like some nice

55

fresh wings? I'll fix 'em myself. On the house," he announced.

From hushed silence to boisterous bliss in a matter of seconds. Matt was impressed at how easily Jake handled the situation. "It won't happen again, Matt, Jake," Carl's friend promised him.

"Maybe I'd better serve Carl a cup of coffee," Matt suggested.

"Good idea." The friend took Carl by the arm and sat him down. "Carl, you're going to drink some coffee now. No more of the hard stuff tonight, you hear?"

Soon, the night picked up again, the happy, carefree atmosphere returning. And Matt continued to rake in the tips. Every so often, he'd pat his apron pocket, the increasing weight a reassuring sign that the bills would be paid and there'd even be a little left over. A new pair of sneakers? Maybe even something special for Julie. It felt great knowing that he had actually earned enough money to say he was supporting a family. Just like the locals, working hard for his money. And it was still only eight o'clock! Matt was sure that by night's end, his other pockets would be stuffed with green, too.

* * *

"Your flight for 9:00 A.M. tomorrow is confirmed, Ms. Sussman. But if the weather is inclement, please be sure to call in the morning to check whether planes are leaving the airport," the woman with the nasal voice said.

"I will. Thank you." Dahlia hung up and reached for the phone book. She'd need a cab to take her to the airport. Once she took care of that, she'd be all set. She just hoped that she could arrange to have her car fixed over the weekend so that she could pick it up on her way back to Ohio after Thanksgiving vacation. *If I get out of this place at all, that is.*

Dahlia lay back on the king-size bed, staring out the window at the blizzard that had dumped nearly a foot of snow on the ground. Inclement weather. With her luck, the blizzard would continue for days, and she'd have to spend her whole vacation here, stuck in the middle of god-knew-where with Nick. The Stargazer Motel. What a joke that was. You couldn't see a thing outside besides solid white.

Why me? she brooded. Maybe if Nick was a little nicer, the prospect of being stuck there wouldn't have seemed half bad. In fact, it might seem awfully cozy, almost idyllic. Stuck with a super-cute guy in a motel room for a few days.

She slipped her bare legs under the covers and pulled the blankets up. At least the steaming hot shower had warmed her up. If she'd had to drive another mile with the busted heater and the window wide open, she would have frozen solid. She wrapped her arms around herself; just thinking about that horrible ride made her shiver all over again.

She glanced toward the bathroom. Steam poured out from the crack between the floor and the bottom of the door. She could hear Nick sighing with relief in the shower. When they had checked in to the room, his teeth were chattering and he was numb from their harrowing ride. Maybe she should have let him take the first shower, she thought. After all, he was the one who had hung out the window for nearly a half hour in the freezing storm, wiping away the snow so that Dahlia could see. He was lucky not to have gotten frostbite.

Well, she was paying for their room. Just letting him use the shower was more than the guy really deserved. But what was she going to do? Leave him out in the snow with only a few dollars in his wallet? She'd considered renting one room for each of them, but then Nick would probably have made some crack about her having money to burn. No, the floor was good enough for him.

She could hear Nick humming in the shower. What a shame, Dahlia thought, picturing the possibilities, that the situation wasn't different. If only she'd kept quiet about her credit cards and rich grandfather. If only Nick hadn't been so darned quick to listen to some stupid rumors on campus in the first place. He had no right to jump to conclusions about her. As she directed a frown at the bathroom door, Dahlia wondered what Nick would think if she told him her big secret.

Yeah, she'd look him right in the eye and say, "Guess who wrote out a big fat check so that Julie could stay in school?"

Would he realize then that he was wrong about her? That she wasn't just a spoiled, selfish, rich kid? Maybe then they could go back to their little dream of driving out west and riding through New Mexico on horseback.

But Nick would probably misinterpret the whole thing. He'd figure she was telling him about paying Julie's tuition just to get his attention or because she felt guilty about being so rich. Or he'd tell her she was trying to buy her friends. And the worst thing would be if word got back to Julie. She might think the same thing. Dahlia would die if Julie found out about the check and felt she owed her anything. No, Dahlia wasn't going to say a word about it to anyone. Especially not to Nick. Some people just didn't understand.

On the wall across from the bed, her image was reflected back in a large mirror. She saw a pretty face framed by long blond hair, and sad blue eyes. She saw a girl who had been through a lot in the past few months and needed a friend, a real friend.

The phone rang. Dahlia reached across the bed for the receiver on the night table. "Hello?"

"Precious, is that you?" her father's voice could be heard over lots of hissing and honking noises.

"Daddy? Where are you? It sounds like you're a million miles from here."

"I'm in the car, Dahlia. Stuck in midtown traffic. We've been caught behind this bus for twenty minutes. And I'm late for a dinner engagement," he complained. Same old Daddy. "What? Just make a U-turn!" she heard him yell, no doubt at a chauffeur who was going to quit in a week as all the others had.

"Daddy?" she repeated into the phone. She wondered if he even remembered why he was returning her call.

"What? Hey, you okay? What happened, anyway? You're supposed to be home by now."

She told her father about the trip home. But her story was punctuated by her father's putting her on hold twice while he took other calls. While she waited for him to return, she could hear Nick finishing up in the bathroom. He had turned off the shower and was whistling.

"Sorry, precious, that was Paris calling," her father said in a hacked voice. "Fashion show. You know. Hey, you'll love the new line we're pushing this year. I'll get you one of everything. Promise. See you tomorrow, right? You'll make it in on time?"

"They say it depends on the weather, Daddy," she said.

"Nonsense. You'll be there. I know you will, precious. Your grandfather can't wait to see you. Got to go. Bye, love."

Dahlia listened to the click on the other end. "Bye," she said softly to herself. *Precious. What a joke.*

The bathroom door opened. Nick was naked, except for a skimpy blue bath towel wrapped around his waist. Actually it must have been the face towel, or maybe the bath mat that the motel had provided, because Dahlia had taken both the big towels for herself. She couldn't help but notice his lean, smooth body. Maybe not as muscular as she remembered Tim's, and not as tan as Andy's, but it was really nice. His torso was long and lean, the full view cut off only by the little towel that he was working hard to make stay on.

Their eyes met only for a second, an awkward second, before Nick quickly looked away. "Where did I put my bag?" he asked nervously. He looked in every direction, except toward the bed next to Dahlia, which is where the yellow gym bag lay.

"Here it is, Nick." Okay, the guy was a jerk. But at least he was a cute jerk. She watched him grab the bag, unzip it, and pull out some clothes, all the time clutching the towel. She wondered how he was going to get his clothes on without the towel falling off.

It was getting hard to stay irritated at such a sight—a handsome guy three-quarters naked in her hotel room. Dahlia was feeling her anger toward him lift dramatically. "My eyes are closed," she said teasingly. Maybe if she lightened up a bit, he would, too, and things between them would ease up. "I won't look. Promise."

But she couldn't keep herself from opening one eye, just a peek, to watch Nick get dressed. She'd never seen someone throw a pair of jeans and a T-shirt on so fast before. She was doing all she could not to giggle.

"Who was that on the phone?" Nick asked. Dahlia could tell he was being careful not to look directly at her. He stood in front of the window, staring out into the swirling blizzard.

"My father. Just making sure I was okay. But if it doesn't stop snowing, my plane won't fly."

"You can always take the bus with me," Nick said stiffly. "Greyhound's like the mailman, rain or snow."

Dahlia sat there, sneaking glances at him staring out the window. He looked sexy, very sexy. She was finally feeling comfortable, warm, relaxed. She wondered how long Nick was going to keep his back toward her.

"Quite a blizzard, huh?" she said. The bed felt cozy. Was it too big for just one person? "Feeling better, Nick?" she asked in a soft voice.

He nodded. "Much. Hey, thanks for paying for the room, Dahlia," he added, sounding friendly enough. Maybe the heat and hot shower were working their spell on him, too,

Dahlia thought. "I appreciate it. And I'll pay you back as soon as I can. Really."

"Don't mention it, Nick. It's my treat, okay?"

"Hey, thanks." His back was still facing her, but Dahlia noticed that both of them were reflected in the window, their faces etched next to each other against the gray-white storm outside.

"Hey, you're welcome," she said, smiling.

Six

❧

"Hey, sexy. Better be careful, or I'm going to gobble-gobble you right up."

"Oooh. I'm scared!" Matt tossed a couple of onions into the shopping cart as Julie gave his arm a love bite.

"Dessert!" She giggled.

"Ow! Julie, I'm trying to shop," he said, laughing. "What's next?"

Julie consulted the list they'd made. "Sweet potatoes, string beans—that's it for vegetables. Oooh, strawberries." She eyed them hungrily, but they were too expensive. "Imported. Well, it *is* November." Instead, she gave a furtive glance around and helped herself to a couple on the spot. "How much have we spent so far?" she mumbled to Matt, her mouth full of the sweet, juicy berries.

Matt did some quick, silent tallying. "Almost twenty dollars. How much more stuff is still on the list?"

"Not much," Julie said. "But don't forget about Tom. He's going to be the most expensive thing."

Matt grinned. "Jules, how're we supposed to cook the guy up when you're calling him by your brother's name?" He put one foot on the rung of the shopping cart, pushed off with the other, and rode it scooter-style down the aisle.

Julie followed him. "Oh, hey, we need toothpaste, don't we?" she said, grabbing a tube of Super Saver's own brand from the sale display at the end of the aisle.

Matt made a face as she tossed it into the cart. "Brand X toothpaste?"

"It's on sale."

Matt reached into the cart and took it out. "Julie, I know we're watching our pennies, but somehow, I just trust Crest in the morning."

Julie shot him a long look. "Wait a minute. Are you practicing for a TV ad or something? Since when do you shop by the label?"

Matt laughed sheepishly. "Look, I know it sounds dumb, but you bought that stuff right after we moved in, and it was gross."

"Are you serious? Matt, it's just toothpaste."

"Jules, brushing my teeth is the first thing I do in the morning. That all-important beginning of my day."

Julie cracked up laughing. A tall, skinny lady with a pinched face pushed her shopping cart by and stared at them. She was one of the few other customers in the store doing some last-minute shopping before the store closed for the holiday. As she turned down the next aisle, Matt did a quick imitation. Julie laughed even harder.

"See, I made you laugh. That's worth the better-tasting toothpaste," Matt said. He put the store brand back on the display rack and went for the Crest.

"Oh, okay," Julie said. "But that means we're going to have to cut out something else."

"Like that fancy shampoo you insisted on?"

"No way!" Julie protested.

"Why can't you just use soap?" Matt asked.

"Just use soap? Matt, don't you love my hair the way it is? So silky smooth."

"Now who's on a TV commercial?"

Still laughing, they pushed their cart up and down each aisle, making sure they had everything. Cranberry sauce, almonds, butter, bread crumbs for stuffing.

"That about does it," Julie said. "Just Tom—I

mean, just the turkey—left." They pushed the shopping cart to the meat counter.

"May I help you?" asked the butcher from behind the high glass meat case.

"Um, yes, we'd like a turkey, please," Julie said.

"What's the name, miss?"

Julie was confused. "The name?"

"Didn't you place an order?" the butcher asked.

Place an order? Julie and Matt looked at each other. "Oops. I guess I forgot that Mom calls up a few weeks in advance," Julie said. She looked down at the meats on display. She didn't see any turkeys. "Don't you have anything left?"

The butcher shrugged. "I got a couple of big guys in the back. Twenty-five, thirty pounders. How many people are you having?"

Julie gulped. "It's just the two of us," she said. A twenty-five-pound turkey was twice the size her mother bought, and they had five for dinner, including her uncle Bob, who ate triple portions.

"We can do up a lot of turkey sandwiches—like for about the next month or two." Matt laughed. "How much is a twenty-five-pound turkey?" he asked the butcher.

"Let's see. At one ninety-nine a pound, it'll come to—"

"A lot," Julie finished for him. She was startled. They'd already spent more than thirty dollars on the other stuff. She looked over at Matt.

"I've only got about forty in my wallet," he said, shaking his head.

"I have ten." Darn. Julie felt the butcher looking at them. Her cheeks got warm.

"Just the two of you, you say?" the butcher asked.

Julie nodded. Once again, she was sadly reminded that Thanksgiving was a holiday for families, for large, happy groups.

"Why don't you try the meat freezer," he said, indicating the long bin full of precut meat. "There ought to be some parts in there. It's still nice, fresh turkey. Cut it up myself."

Julie looked unhappily at Matt. "Where am I going to put the stuffing?" Thanksgiving without her family and without a real stuffed bird.

Matt raised his shoulders. "I made a bundle in tips last night, but you know we've got to bank it to cover the rent." They didn't have any other choice. "Precut Tom," he said wryly, as they slunk off to the meat freezer. "Think it'd help if I put back the Crest?"

Julie gave a little half laugh. "Might buy us an extra wishbone or something."

Matt stopped pushing the cart. "Jules?" He had a serious expression on his face.

Julie felt a beat of alarm. "Yeah?"

"We don't need an extra wishbone." Matt reached for her hand and gave it a squeeze. "I don't know about you, but I have everything I could ever want. Really."

Julie felt her alarm dissolve. She had the sweetest, best guy in the whole world. So what if they didn't have a bird to stuff. Maybe it didn't matter if they ate grilled cheese sandwiches for Thanksgiving dinner. They were really in love, and that was enough to be thankful about.

Marion dabbed a soft white cloth into the pink, creamy silver polish and picked up the gravy boat. She sat at the kitchen table, a pile of silverware in front of her still to be polished. The counters were already overflowing with dishes her mother had spent the whole week preparing: from baked yams to stuffed mushrooms to three kinds of Jell-O molds. There was definitely enough for the small army of relatives who would be arriving shortly.

The smell of Thanksgiving filled the kitchen.

The turkey had been in the oven since early in the morning, and the delicious smell was making everyone hungry. Her two brothers were supposed to be shoveling out a space for the guests to park, but they both kept popping into the kitchen trying to get a jump-start on their meal. Mrs. Green shooed them back outside, warning them that if they began snacking now they'd lose their appetites. "Out," she'd say, threatening to bop them over the head with the ladle she was holding. "We'll be eating soon."

"But, Mom . . ."

"Out!" she ordered. "Unless you'd rather polish silver with your sister."

"No way. Come on, Billy, let's finish shoveling."

Mrs. Green opened up the oven and checked the turkey. "Maybe I was a little hard on them. What do you think, honey?"

"Hmmm?" Marion asked.

"On the boys. I guess I could have given them a bite or two of something."

"They'll be fine," Marion said. She rubbed the gravy boat to a mirrorlike shine.

Her mother came over and sat at the table next to her. She put a hand on Marion's wrist and gave a little squeeze. "Everything okay, dear?"

71

Marion looked up and saw her mom's concerned look. Marion nodded. "Uh-huh."

"No school problems? You sure?"

"I'm sure. I love Madison, really."

"You've been so quiet, sweetie. Ever since you came home yesterday. Your father and I are a little concerned. Aren't you happy to be home, Marion?"

"Of course, Mom. I miss the farm a lot." It was true. Marion was happy to see everybody again. And being around the farm was great. It felt wonderful getting her hands dirty again, milking the cows and feeding the pigs. But Marion knew she couldn't hide anything from her mother. She put the cloth down and shrugged. "It's Fred. He's the boy I told you about last night."

"And at breakfast, and after breakfast," her mother added with a smile. "You like him, that much I can see. But what's the problem, dear?" All of a sudden she let out a big gasp, her eyes and mouth opening wide. "Oh, my goodness, Marion. Oh, no. But you're so young. I mean, you've just met. Oh, don't tell me that you—I mean, you wouldn't . . ."

Marion couldn't keep from laughing. "I wouldn't, so don't worry. But, Mom," Marion protested, "I wouldn't mind a kiss. A real kiss."

Her mother breathed a sigh of relief. "Now, sweetheart, there's no reason to rush into things."

Marion shrugged. "Mom, my friend Julie just got married! And Dahlia has had lots of serious boyfriends, and she's so—so forward about it. I feel like I'm so, I don't know, old-fashioned or something."

"Oh, sweetheart," her mother said soothingly.

"But it's true, Mom. And Fred's so cute, but he's even more shy than I am. It took until yesterday just for a teeny good-bye kiss, and I had to force it on him. It's like he doesn't even know how to pucker up."

"All boys know how to do that." Her mother laughed. "It sounds to me like your friend is a gentleman. When the time is right, you'll both know it." She gave Marion a little hug. "Maybe the two of you just need to find the right place, the right romantic moment. Like your father and I did." She pointed out the window to the snow-covered love swing hanging under the gazebo.

Marion had heard this story about a million times, but she didn't mind hearing it again. "Twenty-five years ago, your father and I sat out there, just two kids without a clue. I had on—"

"A pink and white sundress. And Daddy had on his blue jeans and work shirt," Marion picked up.

"That's right. He had a little rip in the right knee, and he smelled of fresh-cut hay. I remember he kept checking his fingernails to make sure there wasn't any dirt under them. There was, but I didn't care. He said something about finishing his chores early so that we could be together. I just melted into his arms, and we kissed and kissed the whole afternoon."

Marion loved hearing her mother's romantic story. But how were she and Fred going to find themselves in that kind of situation at college? Somehow romance was lacking in her dorm room and the biology lab. And besides, everywhere she and Fred went, there seemed to be a crowd of people around.

The kitchen door opened again, and a rush of cold air swept in along with Marion's brothers. "Did you do the front walk, too?" their mother asked. They shook their heads. She motioned toward the door, and, grumbling, they headed back outside.

"Well, we'd better get back to work, too, Marion. Everyone will be here soon." She got up and returned to the oven to check the turkey. "Oh, sweetie, don't worry so much. You're still young. You have so much to look forward to."

Marion just hoped that something romantic would happen to her while she *was* still young. In the back of her mind, she had a strange image of Fred and her as senior citizens, hunched over, hobbling down the road pushing a baby carriage.

Seven

❧

"Honey, I'm home!" Matt called out teasingly. "P.U. What's burning?"

Julie stood in their little kitchen near tears. The string beans were scorched in a blackened pan on the stove. The wild-rice pilaf was burned on the bottom, too. The sweet potatoes, in a pot of boiling water, were still hard as cement. She was so afraid of what was happening to the turkey parts that she couldn't face opening the oven. And she hadn't even started the gravy yet. About the only thing that hadn't gone wrong was the cranberry sauce—she'd mastered opening the can.

"I ruined everything," she wailed, trying to scrape the charred outside layer off one of the string beans. "I blew Mom's recipe for green beans with almonds."

Matt poked his head into the kitchen. "What's wrong?"

"I don't know. I followed all the instructions." Julie felt like a total failure. How could she have messed up a simple Thanksgiving dinner?

Matt came in and inspected the damage. Julie could see he was trying hard not to make a face. "It doesn't look so bad," he said. "So the beans are a little charcoal-grilled. I love 'em barbecued."

"Matt!"

"Okay. So we won't have the string beans." He lifted the lid from the rice pot. "Uh-oh."

"Or the rice, either," Julie said miserably.

Matt came up from behind and circled his arms around her. "There're always the sweet potatoes. They're my favorite, anyway."

"If they ever cook."

"Turkey?" he asked, as if afraid to hear the answer.

Julie shrugged and opened the oven door. Using a dish towel, she pulled out a baking pan filled with turkey parts. She let out a sigh of relief. They looked okay. On the dry side, but no disaster. Until she cut one of the breasts open. The middle was still red and raw.

"Oh, no. By the time the inside's cooked, the outside will be totally burned."

"Well, aren't you supposed to baste it?" Matt asked. "Keep it moist? Pat was doing the turkeys at work with this thing that looked like a huge eyedropper."

Julie bit her lip. "I *was* basting it. But then all the juices dried up."

Matt took a closer look into the pan. "Oh. That's what that gunky stuff at the bottom is."

Julie couldn't hold back her tears. "Matt, I tried!" She sniffled. "Don't make me feel any worse."

Matt's jaw grew tight. "Julie, relax. I didn't mean it as a criticism. It just slipped out, okay? I mean, I know you've never cooked five dishes at once before."

"And I'm not going to do it again," Julie said, wiping her wet cheeks with the corner of her apron. "Not that we could ever afford to buy more ingredients even if I wanted to."

From the Green, the sound of laughter floated up to their windows. People on their way to or from big holiday dinners. Julie could almost imagine the smell of roasted turkey and the noisy commotion of relatives.

"So it won't be the world's greatest dinner,"

Matt was saying. "But Jake and Pat gave us a pumpkin pie. I put it on the dining room table."

"Great," Julie said unenthusiastically. "We can have pie and cranberry sauce for dinner."

Matt blew out a breath of disappointment. "Okay, so you're not having your perfect family Thanksgiving meal. I'm not partying at the Fast Lane or riding my bike out to the mountains. But hey, we can still light some candles, put on some music. What happened to our romantic celebration for two? So it won't be haute cuisine." He pronounced it "howt."

"Haute," Julie corrected him. "Rhymes with boat and the 'h' is silent."

"Well, ex-*cuse* me," Matt said. "Some of us are out working instead of sitting in Madame What's-her-face's French class. Anyway, I thought she was giving you guys all these tips on cooking in French."

Julie felt the sting of Matt's words. "And what is that supposed to mean?"

"It means that you don't have to make me feel like some dumb jerk just because I'm not a college student. Haute. Does that sound better?" He pronounced it right this time but made an exaggerated snobby expression to go along with it.

Julie was chastened. "Matt," she said more

softly, "I didn't mean to put you down. Anyway, I'm the jerk. I can't even cook dinner." Julie felt as if they were playing grown-up—and failing.

Matt was silent.

"Hey, I'm sorry, okay? I *know* you're out working hard. I *know* you'd rather be taking off for some mountaintop to watch the sunrise. That's why I wanted to make things extra nice —have a really good Thanksgiving meal waiting for you when you got home, like a real family."

Matt frowned. "Jules," he said quietly, "we *are* a real family. We just don't have a lot of practice making holiday dinners and stuff. Yet."

Julie looked at the pan of turkey parts anchored in the goop.

"Julie?" Matt moved forward and cupped her chin in his hands. She met his gaze. "You know what I'd like to do? I'd like to begin all over again. Let's not start our holiday like this." He took a few steps back and took off his leather jacket. "Honey, I'm home," he said.

Julie forced a smile. Right now, Dahlia would be feasting at some chi-chi restaurant in New York City, Marion would be surrounded by dozens of relatives, and Nick would be watching football with his cousins. *That* was a real family.

"Come on," Matt said. "We'll make it nice.

The top layer of the rice looks great, and with some gravy, the turkey will be fine. We'll do the sweet potatoes together. Nice and slowly. What's the rush, anyway? I can think of stuff to do while we wait." He gave her a soft kiss on the forehead. Julie knew Matt meant well.

She put the turkey back in the oven. "Well, I bet the pumpkin pie'll be delicious," she said as brightly as she could. But she couldn't help wishing that tonight, just tonight, she could change places with one of her friends, be a regular college freshman, home for the holidays.

She put her arms around Matt. "Just hold me close," she whispered. *Newlywed.* It sounded so romantic. But sometimes it just felt lonely.

"Happy Thanksgiving!" said the reedy male voice on the other end of the line.

It took Julie a moment to place it. Then she felt a flush of pleasure. "Nick! Hi!" Was he back in Madison early, for some reason? "Where are you?"

"Home. My parents' home, I mean. I just wanted to wish you guys a happy holiday."

Julie smiled. Nick was the sweetest. "That's so nice of you, Nick. Happy Thanksgiving to you, too. How's turkey day going?"

"Oh, okay. The usual. Ate too much, of course. Watched some football with the cousins. It's kind of weird being home again after living on my own. You know, 'Honey, did you wash up before dinner?' 'Son, hadn't you better get down to the station to pick your aunt Margaret up?' 'Nick, that's my seat at the table now.' "

Julie laughed and glanced across the room at Matt. He was picking at the remains of his third slice of pumpkin pie, looking up at her to follow her end of the conversation.

"I think you guys are lucky to be having a mellow holiday by yourselves," Nick went on.

"Mellow. Yeah, I guess you could call it that." Matt was bundled in a heavy sweater, as was Julie, to save on the heating bill, and the only sign of Thanksgiving was the pile of dishes in the sink. Mellow. Well, if that meant the opposite of rowdy, then, sure, they were having a mellow time.

But Julie didn't let on to Nick. He'd called to spread some holiday cheer. And besides, she and Matt were doing their best to pretend to each other that they were having fun. But how many times could you sing the praises of a piece of pie? Julie was happy to get a little break from their somber holiday. She carried the phone over to the table and sat back down.

"So, um, how was your ride home?" she asked as casually as she could. She didn't look up to meet Matt's gaze. He had made it plain enough already that he thought she should butt out. But why shouldn't she want two people she cared about to get to know each other better?

There was a pause at Nick's end. "Well, it was unbelievable, actually," he said. "We almost didn't make it home."

Julie was alert with curiosity. Was Nick telling her what she thought he was? She had a fleeting image of him and Dahlia, parked in her little red car by the side of the road, locked in an embrace. She felt a jolt of surprise, even though it was exactly what she'd been hoping for.

"Her car broke down on us in the snowstorm in the Poconos, and we wound up having to spend the night in a motel."

Julie's surprise deepened. Nick and Dahlia? In a motel? She wanted them to get together, but this seemed awfully quick. Even for Dahlia. "Wow!" she said. *The Poconos.* Julie thought about all those ads she'd seen for romantic weekends in the Poconos. Hotels for lovers only, complete with cozy fireplaces and heart-shaped bathtubs. Leave it to Dahlia to break down in lovers' paradise. "Sounds—cozy!"

Julie looked up at Matt. He arched an eyebrow at her, his interest piqued, despite what he might think of her pushing Nick and Dahlia together. Julie telegraphed him a look of wide-eyed significance.

"Cozy?" Nick was echoing. There was another measured silence. "Look, Julie, I know Dahlia's your best friend, but . . ."

"Oh." Julie frowned, flashing Matt a thumbs-down sign. "Did you have a fight or something?"

"Well, I guess we sort of got off on the wrong foot," Nick confirmed. "I'm sure I wasn't exactly her first choice for someone to get stranded with in the middle of nowhere."

Julie found herself wondering who Nick's first choice *would* be. Or was he still too angry at Allison to think much about other girls? "I'm really sorry," she said to him. She felt a little guilty. "I suppose it's kind of my fault." Maybe Matt had been right about not getting involved.

"Hey, no big deal," Nick said easily. "I mean, once we got used to the idea that we weren't going anyplace, we both tried to behave ourselves a little better. You know, kind of overly polite."

"Well, maybe the trip back'll be better," Julie said uncertainly.

"No question about that," Nick said. "I'm taking the bus. Alone."

"Oh. That bad, huh?" So much for the return trip.

"Her car's still in Pennsylvania. She's got to pick it up, assuming they can fix it over the weekend," Nick explained. "Flying there—of course. Probably right to the gas station if old Gramps Sussman can arrange it."

So that's it. Julie was starting to get the picture. She blew out a breath of disappointment. "Nick, she's not really what you think. I mean, maybe on the surface, but underneath she's really a great person. Give her a chance. You just have to get to know her."

"Maybe," Nick said noncommittally. "I mean, I'm sure that's true, since she's your friend, but—well, I just don't think she's used to thinking about anyone else before herself. I mean we get into the motel totally frozen, and she hogs the shower for about a half an hour and then uses all the big towels."

Julie laughed. "Serious crime, Nick."

Nick laughed, too. "I guess that sounds kind of petty. But look, if it had been you and me in that motel, you wouldn't have done that."

Julie felt herself getting warm. Her and Nick in a motel together? "Different strokes. Variety is the spice of life," she said quickly. "Not that we know anything about cooking around here," she added, changing the subject. "We learned that lesson tonight."

She told Nick about her kitchen fiasco.

"But you had the pie," he commented at the end of her story. "We had the yearly nightmare from Aunt Sydney's oven—tastes like old road kill, but you have to tell her how good it is, and then she forces seconds on you." Julie couldn't stop laughing as Nick did a series of impressions of his various relatives and the Thanksgiving scene at his family's house.

"Wow, it's really nice to talk to you," she said as the conversation finally wound down. "I miss you."

"Same," Nick said. "Hey, you want to put your other half on? Let me say hi to him?"

"Definitely. See you in a few days, Nick. Bye." Julie smiled at Matt across the table and passed him the phone.

"Hey, man! How's it going?" Matt asked.

Julie got up and began clearing away their dishes. As she stacked the plates in the little kitchen sink, she could hear Matt talking and laughing.

"I can't believe you bet on the Cowboys. What are you, nuts?" He paused. "Yeah, well, we'll get the hang of that home cooking thing eventually."

Julie smiled. She was glad her two favorite guys got along so well. It was important to her that Matt had some friends in Madison, that he was starting to feel more at home.

Too bad about Nick and Dahlia, though. Julie just wanted them both to have someone special.

Eight

✣

Dahlia sat in the burgundy and jade dining room of the Szechuan Palace with her old gang from high school. All five of them were at "their" table by the window, looking out at the busy Manhattan street. Dahlia remembered spending major amounts of time there during high school, eating lunch or just plain hanging out, drinking Chinese tea, skipping classes, and watching the rest of the world go by.

It was like old times, being back in New York, hanging out with her old pals. A trio of briefcase-carrying businessmen marched across the street, ignoring the blinking Don't Walk sign. All three wore long, heavy wool overcoats. A woman in a full-length fur walked a tiny French poodle. Three kids on skateboards whizzed up Third Avenue in the middle of traffic. *Same as it ever was,* Dahlia thought. *Same as it ever was.*

"A toast," said Jacqueline, holding up her glass. Jacqueline, who'd moved to New York from Paris in junior high, was always toasting something. Her new Porsche, a midwinter trip to the Bahamas for that perfect tan, a cute guy —it didn't matter. There was always plenty to celebrate. Dahlia raised her glass automatically, along with the others. "To high school," Jacqueline proclaimed. "Thank God we're out of there!" Everyone clinked glasses and sipped.

"And another toast," Dahlia added, raising her glass again. "To all of us being together again back in the city. I missed you guys. Even you, Thadd," she said, tipping her glass toward him and giving him a playful wink. Thadd, Dahlia's ex from senior year, still looked cute, especially suntanned and with a recently dyed purple streak in the middle of all his long, blond hair.

"Missed me, huh? I'm not surprised," Thadd said, flirting back. "No, really. I missed you guys, and the city and all, too. But life down south is awesome. The sun. Amazing. Incredible frat parties, the most beautiful girls in the world—and lucky me, they all love me!"

Yep, same old Thadd. Dahlia was reminded

of the many reasons why she was glad he had chosen a college a thousand miles away from Madison.

"If you think there's fun in the sun in North Carolina, Thadd, you wouldn't believe UCLA. You've got to wear SPF fifteen in the library. Seriously," Liz said. "Seeee-riously," she repeated with emphasis. Dahlia laughed, but it was about the tenth time already today that Dahlia had heard her say that word. It was starting to get to her—seriously!

"I can't believe you came home from California just for Thanksgiving break, Liz. Bet your dad flew you first class, too." Marcus Wellington snickered.

"What's the big deal?" she shot back. "Daddy missed me. Why wouldn't he fly me first class?"

"Well, *I* took the *bus* back from Dartmouth, with the regular people." Marcus, another of Dahlia's exes, had grown a mustache and a funny little goatee. Barely grown one, actually. While he talked, Dahlia couldn't help but notice the patches of clean, white skin that refused to sprout hairs. "Paid the forty bucks myself," he boasted.

"Marcus on a bus? Marcus J. Wellington the Third on a bus. Imagine that," Dahlia teased. "I hope you won't have to smash your piggy bank to pay for the return trip."

"Really, like the silver piggy bank in the palace," Liz added. "I mean, seeee-riously, Marcus, give us all a break, will you? I bet you had the driver drop you off at your door."

Dahlia laughed heartily with the others. Even she was poor compared to Marcus. It seemed as if his father owned about half the real estate on the Upper East Side of Manhattan, including the building that Dahlia had grown up in. Dahlia remembered how when she was dating him, he'd send a limousine all of four blocks to pick her up and bring her back to his place.

"You guys don't have to be so harsh on me," Marcus protested. "She's the one who flew in from L.A."

"It wasn't my idea to come back for five days," Liz said. "I had plans to do Yosemite with Alex. Tents, sleeping bags. You know, the western thing. But as soon as I told my dad it was just the two of us, you know what he said? 'Only if you'd like to be disinherited!' Like what's the difference between being together in the dorm or in a sleeping bag?" She shrugged.

"So your dad knows you're sleeping with this guy?" Jacqueline asked.

"Well . . . not exactly," Liz admitted, to more raucous laughter.

Dahlia's laughter, however, was only half-hearted. Liz's story reminded her of her and Nick's New Mexico fantasy—before things turned so sour between them. Horses, mountains, sunsets. "The West Coast thing," as Liz had put it.

Nick. Here Dahlia sat, in a restaurant on the plush Upper East Side of Manhattan with her childhood pals talking jets, bank accounts, and glitz. Nick, meanwhile, was serving food in a soup kitchen, maybe even right around the corner from where Dahlia was.

It wasn't the first time Dahlia had thought about him since she'd gotten home. He'd been an invisible presence while Grampa Sussman was passing out the holiday checks the day before, and while her parents were rambling on about their trip to Greece and their upcoming scuba-diving expedition in Australia. Invisible, maybe, but disapproving nonetheless. Dahlia knew Nick would have been turned off by her whole New York scene. But that was *his* problem, wasn't it? If he couldn't relate to her, so what? Then why was he still on her mind?

The balding Chinese waiter brought a huge tray of steaming dishes to their table. With a gracious smile, he put each platter down on the lazy Susan in the middle of the table. "Everybody have big feast again today," he said. "Second Thanksgiving. Chinese Thanksgiving, today."

Rather than just say thanks, Marcus made a gagging motion. "Blah. I'm still stuffed from yesterday. Why do we always have to order so much food here?"

" 'Cause it's yummy. We don't have to finish it, Marcus," Liz said. "Pass the noodles."

"Why not give the leftovers to those 'regular' people you met on the bus?" Jacqueline suggested. Dahlia watched all her friends break into hysterics. But suddenly she didn't find much to laugh about. Nick in a soup kitchen and her friends acting as if they owned the planet.

Dahlia didn't remember her high school gang always sounding this obnoxious. Had they gotten worse? Dahlia remembered telling Julie how much she loved all her New York pals. Now she was just glad that Julie wasn't with her to hear the conversation. *Or Nick,* she thought. She could barely imagine what his reaction to her friends would be.

Dahlia helped herself to a serving of cold noodles with sesame sauce, managing her chopsticks with expertise. She passed Marcus the bowl.

Marcus shook his head. "Aren't you stuffed from last night?"

"Hardly. I hate the food at Tavern on the Green. You know, the Tavern is all style," she said. "We had about ten different courses of things I couldn't even pronounce, and a different wine for each course. They just kept serving me the next dish before I even touched the one I had in front of me."

"Wow, it must have cost a fortune," Jacqueline said. "I would have traded places with you in a sec. We had the typical American meal at home. Turkey, cranberry sauce, sweet potatoes, and stuffing with gravy. Gross. Like my parents feel they have to make up for being French. Check it out, we even had American wine and apple pie for dessert."

"So did we," Dahlia said. "Only they called it *tarte aux pommes.* And it tasted like toilet paper. Pass the shrimp, Thadd."

"You're really funny, Dahlia," Liz said. "Seeeriously funny." She dug into the shrimp with broccoli. "So, Jacqueline, how's life at B.U.?"

"Pretty good, except that it's so overcrowded this year. All the freshmen have to live in triples," Jacqueline said.

"Triples?" Liz said. "So what happens when . . ."

"We took care of that one. We've got this elaborate warning system so that no one will get disturbed. The only problem is when you have to wait an hour till, well, you know. And no sleepovers, because then the other two would never get to go to bed."

"How about you, Dahlia?" Marcus asked. "Do you have the triple problem? I bet that would drive you crazy."

Dahlia shot him a glare. "And what's that supposed to mean?"

"Come on, Dahlia. Lighten up. I just figured there must be tons of guys out there who'd go wild over somebody like you. It's a compliment, okay?"

"Hey, what about Paul Chase?" Jacqueline asked. "You were half the reason he went to Madison, Dahlia."

"Seee-riously," Liz whined. "Any sparks yet?"

"Yeah, but not the kind you're thinking of," Dahlia said. "We had a little—a little misunderstanding." She figured that was about all they needed to know about her and Paul.

"So what about the rest of the guys at Madison?" Marcus pressed. "Don't think for a second that we're going to believe you were Miss

Virtue all semester. Come on, Dahlia, they must love you in Ohio."

"You're gross, Marcus. But if you really want to know, they do love me. And I have my own room, too, so I don't have to run around putting little signs up when I want my privacy."

"A single? Wow! Lucky you. How did you swing that one?" Liz asked. "Pay double, or something?"

"No, I had a roommate. Julie. She's really great. But she got married in the middle of the semester."

Jacqueline's mouth dropped open. "Huh?"

"Married? Like 'with this ring I thee wed'? I don't get it. Wasn't she a freshman, too?" Thadd asked.

"Yep. I know it sounds weird. I couldn't figure it out at first either," Dahlia said. "Her high school boyfriend came out from Philadelphia, and the next thing you know, they were Mr. and Mrs. Or Mr. and Ms. Whatever. It was pretty wild. But they're really happy together."

"Yeah? Sounds like a drag to me," Thadd said. "Didn't you tell her she'd miss out on all the fun? What about the one-hunk-per-week rule?"

"Really," Jacqueline agreed. "The more, the merrier. I mean I want to get married, too—

someday. Mega-wedding at the Plaza. But not during college."

"Actually, Julie and Matt are great together," Dahlia said, sticking up for her friends. She realized, as she spoke, that she really meant it, too. "Yeah, they're totally in love. It's kind of cool, you know? Like it was meant to be."

"It'll probably only last a few months," Thadd said. "Dumb idea."

"So was there a party and everything?" Marcus asked. "Did you get to be the maid of honor?"

Dahlia shook her head. "I guess I kind of wish I had been, though. But they eloped. Totally romantic, you know? Like the movies. They rode into the sunset on his Harley. Julie was wearing this really cool antique dress that she and I bought at a thrift shop."

"So what did her parents say?" Liz asked. "They must have seer-iously flipped. Send your daughter out to school, inherit a son-in-law."

"Yeah, they flipped all right. Her dad even cut off her funds." *Ooops.* Dahlia wished she hadn't said that. The last thing she meant to do was tell her friends that she was the one who had paid Julie's tuition bill. They'd probably have her arrested for spreading some of the wealth.

"Her parents really cut her off? Like disinherit?" Marcus asked.

"She isn't a rich kid, if that's what you mean. It just means that she and Matt have to work a little harder to pay the bills. But it's cool, they're happy together. Seeee-riously," she said, turning to look at Liz.

"If you say so," Liz responded with a shrug. "Sounds awfully stale, though."

Dahlia skewered one of her shrimp with her chopstick. Maybe she shouldn't have expected them to understand. It seemed that all they could relate to were suntans in the middle of winter and jets across the country for the weekend.

Dahlia knew she hadn't acted too differently when she'd started college. But she felt as if things were starting to change. She took a deep breath. She had a lot to think about, a lot to work out. She was even starting to feel ready to go back.

Nine

❧

Julie got under the covers Sunday night and reached down for the Agatha Christie mystery on the floor near the bed. It sure was nice not to have much schoolwork for a few days, she thought. Next to her, Matt lay flipping through the latest issue of *Sports Illustrated*. He poked an arm out from the covers and circled it around her shoulder without looking away from the article he was reading.

Julie snuggled up to him, feeling his warmth through her nightgown. It might not have been the perfect Thanksgiving weekend, but they'd managed to have some good times anyway. There had been the walk in the snow that had turned into a serious snowball fight, and their ride on the motorcycle out to Lake Erie, stopping for hot chocolate on the way back. Saturday they'd gone ice skating at the Madison rink before Matt had to go to work. As for their Thanksgiving dinner itself, it was bound to be better next year. Julie kissed Matt's bare shoulder.

Still, Julie wasn't sorry that Thanksgiving break was almost over. Earlier in the evening, she had heard plenty of raucous shouts and greetings out on Main Street as students called to one another across Madison Green. Marion had called to say that she and most of the kids on Julie's old hall were back already and everyone else was on their way. By Monday, all Julie's friends would have returned to campus. It had been a little lonely in Madison without them. Maybe more than a little.

Now Julie opened her book and tried to find her place. Where was she? The part where the dead man's brother was about to—

"Noooo!" From somewhere outside, a shriek penetrated the closed windows of their little apartment.

Julie froze, her body seized with fear. Matt lowered his magazine, and their eyes met. Another scream pierced the air.

"Hey," Julie whispered. "What's going on out there?

"Must be somebody fooling around," Matt

said, although he sounded nervous. They both sat poised for the third scream.

"No! Leave me alone! *Stop!*" shrieked a terrified girl's voice.

Matt threw down his magazine and jumped out of bed. Julie raced out into the living room after him. They rushed to the window and pressed their faces to it, looking out onto the dimly lit town green. The screams continued, but Julie couldn't tell where they were coming from. The walkways that crisscrossed Madison Green were illuminated by old-fashioned street-lamps sending out hazy pools of yellow light, but the broad stretches of grass were dark, except for an occasional patch of snow left over from the storm.

"Matt?" Julie felt her pulse racing. "Someone's in trouble! We've got to do something!"

Matt ran back into the bedroom and grabbed a pair of pants, tossing Julie the clothes she'd just taken off and thrown over a chair. They were dressed in record time, pulling on their jackets as they ran down the stairs, out the door, and across the Green.

Julie pumped her legs as hard as she could as they followed the screams toward the campus side of the Green. Her breath coming fast and hard in the cold air, she thought she saw a shadowy figure ahead of her and over to her right. "Matt! Over there," she shouted.

As her voice pierced the night, she saw a man's silhouette sprinting away from them. On the ground was a smaller figure. They raced over. A girl lay on the ground, her feet in a patch of snow, her face buried in her hands in the mud-soaked grass. Her ski jacket was torn, and her shirt was pushed up around her shoulders. Julie could hear her crying.

The night-shrouded outline of the man was growing smaller. "Wait here!" Matt said, taking off after him.

Briefly, Julie watched him go, then knelt down toward the girl on the ground. "It's okay," she said softly. She reached a hand out and gently touched her arm. The girl flinched. "I'm not going to hurt you," Julie said.

The girl raised herself into a sitting position and pushed her thick, wavy hair out of her face. Julie gasped. "Sarah!" Her heart beat crazily. It was Sarah Pike from her old dorm!

"Julie!"

"Sarah, are you all right? What happened? What did he do?"

Sarah pulled down her shirt and zipped her jacket, then crossed her arms and hugged herself tightly. "I'm okay," she said, rocking back and forth. "I'm okay." But she was in tears.

"Did he—" Julie's unfinished sentence hung in the night air.

Sarah shook her head. "I think you guys scared him off before he had a chance . . ."

Julie looked in the direction Matt had gone, but all she saw across from the Green were the familiar buildings of Madison College, their outer walls lit like a stage set, and a frighteningly quiet campus. Suddenly Julie felt isolated and scared. "Who was he, Sarah? Did you get a good look?"

Sarah shot Julie a frightened, skittish glance. She looked down at the ground. Then she shook her head hard. "I didn't see him. No. No, I didn't see a thing."

"Well, he's not going to hurt you now," Julie said softly. "It's going to be all right." She hoped her voice didn't betray how nervous she felt. "Thank God you're okay." She reached out for Sarah again, and this time Sarah didn't pull away.

As Julie hugged her and repeated her words of reassurance, the wail of a siren and the flash of lights came speeding toward them from the direction of town. "Here. They're coming to help us," she said, feeling her own relief. Her gaze followed the police car as it turned up Center Street and came to a screeching halt at the edge of the Green nearest to them. Two police officers jumped out of the car and ran toward them, the lights of the patrol car still throwing a strobe of blue and red on the tree trunks and the buildings.

"We got a call someone needed help out here," the taller, older officer said, dropping down next to Julie and Sarah. "Anyone hurt?"

"Yes, sir," Julie said. "There's been—my friend was—attacked. A man tried to—to rape her," she said, forcing the ugly word out of her mouth. She felt horrified all over again, the word bringing home the terror of the deed.

"Tried? So nothing happened," the second officer asked.

"Nothing?" Julie felt her voice rise with protest. "My friend was attacked—Officer."

"Will you let her talk for herself, miss?" he said without emotion.

The first policeman looked up at him. "Jim, I'll handle this. It would be helpful if the young lady told us her story in her own words," he said.

Sarah sniffled and wiped at her eyes with a muddy glove. "I was just walking home," she said. "And this guy jumped on me. I didn't even see him coming. I tried to get him off of me. I tried . . ."

Julie felt the horror of being knocked down by a shadowy form. Of struggling under his weight.

"He—he tried to get my clothes off. I couldn't stop him," Sarah went on. "Then he must have seen Julie coming."

The older officer nodded and took out a pad. He jotted down a few notes. "And your name is—?"

"Sarah."

"Last name?"

"Pike."

"Okay, Miss Pike," he said gently. "You were going home. Which is—"

"Wilson Hall. That's my dorm," Sarah said. Julie nodded at her encouragingly.

"And where were you coming from?"

Julie saw Sarah stiffen. "The library," she said, after a moment's pause.

"The school library?"

She nodded.

"All the way on the other side of campus? I thought it was closed for vacation."

"I just had to return a book. I put it into the book deposit."

105

"At midnight?" the officer asked, a note of skepticism creeping into his voice.

"Well, if you'd let me finish . . ." Sarah snapped, her voice wavering as if she was about to start crying again.

Out of the corner of her eye, Julie saw someone approaching. She looked over. Matt! At the same time, she saw the younger officer move his hand to his holster.

"He's my husband!" she shouted, her heart in her throat. The police officer let his hand drop. Julie took a deep breath.

Matt came over, shaking his head. "I lost him," he said. "I thought I was fast, but he was—" He left his sentence hanging. "Sarah. Oh, no."

"It's all right, Matt," Julie said. "We scared him off before he could really hurt her."

"Miss Pike was telling us what happened," the first officer prompted. "So after dropping your book off you did what?"

Sarah's lip trembled. "Can't I just go home?" she said. "I want to go home and forget about it."

"As soon as you finish telling us what happened," he assured.

Sarah sighed. "Well, after the library, I went over to my brother's house, okay? He was having some friends over, and he invited me to come by."

"Your brother's name?"

Sarah was silent. This had to be so awful for her, Julie thought, to be interrogated on top of what had just happened.

"Tim," Sarah answered, barely able to talk. "Look, can't you just leave him out of it?" she pleaded. "I don't want anyone asking me any more questions. Not him and not you. I just want to forget this ever happened, don't you understand?" She was shaking. Julie put an arm around her.

"Of course we understand. But you want to catch this guy, don't you?" Julie asked.

Sarah shrugged.

"Of course you do. But, Officer, she said she didn't see what he looked like," Julie said.

"But you did." The officer turned to Matt.

Matt shook his head. "Only from the back, sir. He was a big guy, and he was real fast. Ski jacket. I couldn't see what color it was. I'm afraid I can't give you any more information."

The policeman nodded and wrote everything down. "Local? College student?" he asked Matt.

Julie saw Matt's jaw go tight. "How do you expect me to know that?" he asked angrily.

"Matt," Julie said, embarrassed. She knew

what Matt was thinking: local, student, why should it make a difference? Still, this was a police officer Matt was talking to.

"Excuse me," he said, a little more calmly. "Look, like I said before, I hardly got a glimpse of the guy. It was dark."

The officer just sighed. "I thought perhaps from the way he was dressed. . . . I just want to get my hands on the guy and make sure he doesn't cause any more trouble."

"I understand, sir," Matt muttered.

"Okay. Now, you'll have to give me your names," he said to Julie and Matt, "and then we'll take Miss Pike home."

"Sarah, we'll go with you, if you want," Julie said. She still couldn't believe that this had happened to someone she knew.

Sarah looked at her with moist eyes. She nodded. "Yeah. Thanks, Julie. But then—then just forget anything ever happened, okay? That's what I'm going to do."

"Sure, Sarah," Julie said, but she knew that forgetting about it would be impossible for both of them.

Ten

❧

Later that night, after Julie and Matt had gone with the police to take Sarah back to the dorm, they returned to the safety of their little apartment. Once inside, Matt took Julie in his arms and held her tight. He could feel her body tremble, feel her sobs of fright. "Shhh. It's okay, Jules. It's going to be all right. Shhh," he whispered, even though he was shaking, too.

Ugly world, he thought. *Ugly world.* Poor Sarah. In the wrong place at the wrong time. But at least something even worse hadn't happened.

"Matt," Julie cried. "Why?"

"Shhhh. It's over, sweetheart." He couldn't help thinking that it could have been Julie out there. She'd walked across the Green alone plenty of times. And whoever was lurking there could have just as easily found another victim. Matt and Julie's happiness suddenly seemed so vulnerable. He kept a strong, protective hold on Julie, the most precious person in his life.

"It's not fair," Julie managed between sobs. "It's just not fair."

"I know, Julie. I know." The fragility in Julie's voice instantly reminded Matt of how she'd been after Mary Beth's and Mark's accident. That one made even less sense than this. At least Sarah was alive.

"What are we going to do, Matt?" Julie asked weakly.

"I don't know, Julie. Just try to relax, huh? Hold on to me." He pulled her closer. "And don't forget how much I love you. Don't forget that."

"I love you, too, Matt." Julie's face was pressed against his.

"You've got to try to forget it. Like Sarah said. Let's just try to forget."

"Forget? How can I?"

As he held her, Matt ran through the last hour in his head. The screams, the call for help. He remembered racing down the stairs. Was he fast enough? If only he'd gotten there a moment sooner he might have been able to catch up with the guy. *Why wasn't I faster?* he thought.

And that cop. What difference had it made to him if the guy was a townie or a student? Why was everybody so hung up about the town-gown thing anyway?

All of a sudden, Matt thought about the scene in the Barn and Grill from the other night. *"Sweet Julie. Sweet, sweet Julie. . . . Does sweet Julie have a friend for me, man? Sure, she does. A fine young* college *girl just waiting to meet ole Carl."* A horrible thought invaded Matt's mind. But, no, it couldn't be.

"What is it, Matt?" Julie asked as his body tensed up. "What's wrong?"

"Nothing. I was just thinking about this thing that happened the other night at work. It's nothing. Really."

Julie wiped away her tears as she looked up at him. "I can tell it's something, Matt. What?"

"It's just something this guy at the Barn and Grill said," he admitted. He told her about Carl's lewd, drunken remarks and his stupid threats.

"Why didn't you say something about that sooner, Matt?" Julie asked. "He sounds scary."

Matt shrugged. "I don't know. The guy's always talking trash. No one ever seems to take him seriously. It was just drunken jabber. I used to hear it all the time at the Fast Lane. It's the same everywhere. You know, a guy has a few too many, and he starts in. Believe me, his talk is way bigger than his bite."

" 'I'm gonna get me one'? You think that's just jabber?"

"Come on, Julie. You remember my dad's club on Friday nights. People like to mouth off about what's bothering them. Carl's just angry about being a townie on a college campus. He happened to have had a partial audience that night at the Barn and Grill, so he went a little overboard."

"A little? He made dangerous threats," Julie said. "You should have told the police, Matt."

Matt released his hold on Julie. He could see the wheels turning in her head, and he didn't like where they were going. "Julie, you weren't there, so you don't know what he really meant."

"And you do?"

"Look, Jules. I know the guy. He's in there almost every night. I don't like him too much, but he's not the one who I was chasing out there on the Green."

"How can you be sure?" Julie asked. "You told the police you barely saw the guy. I really don't understand why you didn't tell them about Carl."

"Because I wasn't thinking about him. Not

112

with Sarah lying on the ground. Anyway, even if I had thought about Carl, I probably wouldn't have said anything. If I had squealed, the cops probably would have just jumped to false conclusions. You heard the way they instantly assumed it was a townie. If I had just mentioned Carl's name, they would have gone and bothered him for nothing."

"Nothing? Nothing?!" Julie's voice rose in anger. "Is that what you think just happened out there?" She stepped away and folded her arms tightly. Matt felt his own temper beginning to come alive, too. "And if we didn't get there in time, Matt? Who knows? Sarah could have . . . she could have been killed. And if it was that guy—"

Matt held his breath for a moment, trying to keep himself from exploding. "For the last time, Julie, it wasn't Carl. He just got a little too drunk that night, that's all. If Carl wanted to go out with a college girl, I'm sure he'd ask her. He wouldn't force her. Now come on, Jules." Matt reached for her hand, trying to stop the fight before it got any more out of control. "I thought we were both on the same side here. You're just upset, Jules. We both are. Maybe we should just try and relax and not think about it."

113

But Julie refused to let it go. "The police should at least have gone to his house. Just to make sure he was asleep. The townies might hate us, but they don't have the right to just go and—"

"And attack college girls? So you've decided it was a local, too?" Matt yelled, pulling his hand away.

There was a stone-cold silence. Then Matt said, "I can't believe you're so quick to condemn him. Hang him with no proof."

"I didn't say that, Matt." Her voice sounded so disapproving, so hard.

"You just refuse to see that the college students around here treat this place like it's their own personal Disneyland. Madison's one big playground where nothing bad could ever happen. Sarah walking around by herself in the middle of the night. She wouldn't do that at home. Well, wake up, it's the real world here, too. Even in little Madison, Ohio, life can be dangerous. Just like everywhere else."

Julie threw her hands up in the air. "So now you're saying it's her fault?" She backed up against the living room window, the dark, deserted Green outside, behind her. "I suppose you think she deserved it, too. We college kids need a slap in the face every once in a while, is that it? Just to remind us that life stinks." She turned away from him, but he could hear her start to cry.

"I didn't say that at all. Julie? Look at me." But she wouldn't turn around. She just shook her head and stared out the window. In the dim reflection, Matt could see the tears still flowing.

He didn't know what to do next. This was awful. They were both so on edge about Sarah that everything they said just made it worse. Matt wasn't even sure he'd meant half of what he'd just said. "Maybe we should just go to bed. Maybe a good night's sleep . . ."

But Julie kept shaking her head. "I can't sleep. It's too awful," she mumbled through the tears. "Poor Sarah."

Matt walked over to her and put a tentative hand on her shoulder. He could feel her tense muscles. "You've got to try to calm down, Jules."

"How am I supposed to be calm after what happened tonight? Especially with that guy out there somewhere." He felt her shiver.

"Julie, forget about Carl!" Matt couldn't control his shout.

"I meant the guy who attacked Sarah!" Her voice level topped Matt's. She whipped her head around, shooting him an incensed glare.

"Whoever he is. And I don't care what you say, it could be Carl."

"You're saying that just because he's a townie. Just because he wears the scarlet letter that says he's a regular guy who goes to work instead of plays in school." Matt was sorry the instant the words were out of his mouth, but he knew the damage was done.

"Play?" Julie's rage intensified. "Is that what you think I do in school? Play?"

"Look, I didn't mean that, but if you want to know how I really feel, I think that everybody, including you, blows the town-gown rift way out of proportion. You guys are good, and we're all bad. Even the cops are on your side. They know where the money comes from around here. It's all a bunch of crap."

"Us guys, you guys? I didn't know we'd taken sides, Matt. You're the one who's decided you're a townie."

"Well, I'm sure not a college student!" Now it was Matt who stepped away. He and Julie had never fought like this before. It was so ugly. Matt felt more distance between them than when he was still back in Philadelphia.

Any attempt at words was a failure. Matt found himself pacing the little apartment. The main room was barely big enough for two when they were friends. He wanted out. He needed space. He began walking toward the front door. But the thought of leaving Julie alone after what had happened to Sarah stopped him in his tracks. He wanted to be anywhere but in that apartment, but he couldn't leave.

Julie had slumped down into the leopard-skinned armchair. Matt could feel her eyes following him. He just couldn't continue the fight. Not now. He went into the bedroom and slammed the door shut.

Julie fought for a breath of air as she was hurled down. She opened her mouth, trying to get her lungs to work as she simultaneously struggled to get off the ground.

Boom! She was thrown down again, a huge, shadowy, faceless figure throwing his weight on top of her. She waved her arms and legs uselessly, pinned to the ground by him. As she struggled to get free, there was an explosion of metal and glass in her ears, and suddenly she was imprisoned, not by some attacker, but in the crumpled, burning wreckage of Mary Beth's car. Smoke, fire, an inferno blazed around her. Escape—she had to get free. She had to—

Her eyes flew open as she slipped off the

armchair and landed on the floor with a hard thud. She gasped for air. There was sweat on the back of her neck and her upper lip, and her heart was pumping with fear. What was she doing here? Where was Matt?

She remembered the fight. Matt slamming the bedroom door. She'd fallen asleep crying, right here in the armchair in the living room. And then, the nightmare.

She inhaled deeply, slowly and deliberately. It was only a nightmare. Suddenly her muscles tensed again. Only a nightmare for *her*. But for Sarah the terror had been real.

Forget about what had happened? Impossible. And Julie knew that no matter what Sarah said, she wouldn't forget either. She'd live and relive the horror: What had happened. What could have happened. Even if she refused to talk about it, the fear would stay bottled up inside.

Julie got up and went into the bathroom. She took her bathrobe off the hook on the inside of the bathroom door and wrapped it around herself. She padded across the threadbare rug in the living room to the windows. Outside, the Green looked so quiet, so peaceful. The gazebo in the middle of it was like a monument to the perfect little American town. Or at least it looked that way. Was the attacker out there somewhere waiting for his next chance?

Julie turned away from the window. How could she go back to sleep? Sarah's screams were too fresh in her mind, and her own nightmare lurked at the fringes of her imagination.

She looked around for her shoulder bag and found it under one of the chairs in the kitchen. She pulled a notebook out of it, then felt around in the bottom of the bag for a pen. She knew it would help if she wrote down what she was feeling. She'd done it ever since she was a little girl, whenever something was weighing on her mind. She sat down at the table and uncapped her cartridge pen. This was the best way to understand her fears better, to get them off her chest.

At midnight I heard a terrifying scream outside my window, she wrote. *By the time I got there, the night was silent.* She filled the page with her round, slanted handwriting, recounting what had happened to Sarah and how Sarah had seemed so afraid to tell what had happened to her. *She wanted to cover up the horror as if to say it didn't really happen—even if it meant covering up her attacker's crime.*

Julie poured her thoughts and feelings into her notebook: about women, afraid to speak their minds; about women who were supposed to hope their problems would just go away. *Calm down, forget about it,* Julie wrote. *That's what we're supposed to do.*

Even Matt, she thought, her pen poised in midair, had told her to relax. Relax! After what had happened.

She began to write again: about men who felt free to say whatever they wanted; about the man in the Barn and Grill. *He had no problem making lascivious remarks. The kind that lead to screams in the middle of the night,* Julie wrote. *Yet my friend was afraid to speak out. Why? Because someone might think she did something to deserve it? Because she felt somehow ashamed? Until women can speak as freely as men, this sort of horror will continue to be covered up, brushed under the rug, and repeated over and over.*

She leaned back in her chair and reread what she had written. Already, the events of the night were loosening their grip on her—the terrifying scene on the Green, her fight with Matt, her nightmare. It helped to get her feelings down on paper, kind of like a personal version of the op-ed articles they were writing in journalism class, where people aired their views on important events. Maybe Professor Copeland, awful as he was, was actually teaching her something after all.

Julie wondered, for a moment, what he'd think about what she'd written. She frowned. He'd probably return it to her covered with biting comments in red pen. Copeland wasn't very big on women's issues. He was the kind of person who probably thought women should be seen and not heard.

Julie felt herself getting angry. It was precisely what she'd put down on paper. Women being afraid to speak out. Hiding, keeping it all inside. Of course, Julie should let Professor Copeland know what she thought. She should tell him and everyone else in Madison, town and college alike. After all, didn't this concern all of them?

She bent over her notebook again, and an hour or so later she had turned her nighttime thoughts into a well-versed, thoroughly thought-out article. She finished up by taking out Sarah's name to protect her privacy. She reread it twice more and then carefully tore the pages out of her notebook, folding them in half and putting everything away in her bag. Tomorrow, she'd type up her article and deliver it in person to the Madison *Register*. Maybe it would even make it to print.

Julie smiled for the first time all night. She turned out the lights and let herself into the bedroom. Matt was sleeping on his back, mouth slightly open, a lock of dark hair falling over his forehead. Julie slipped off her bathrobe, let it fall to the floor, then got into bed. She felt Matt rolling over toward her.

"What? Julie? Is that you? Where've you been?" he mumbled, three-quarters asleep.

"Nowhere. Just in the living room. Shhh," Julie whispered. Now that she'd gotten everything off her chest, she felt a lot better about him, too. She really did know how hard it was for him in Madison, not fitting in one place or the other. Under the covers, she circled one arm around his waist. He was soft and warm with sleep.

Matt snuggled closer. "Jules?"

"Go back to sleep," Julie said, kissing him softly on the cheek.

"Okay," Matt said, his voice rough with sleep. "But, Julie, I'm sorry we fought."

Julie smiled. "Me, too, Matt." She held him in her arms as he fell back to sleep. As the first weak signs of daylight filtered in through the bedroom window, she was still watching him.

Eleven

❧

"Come on, guys! Give it a rest," Dahlia moaned to herself, opening one eye and looking at her alarm clock. Seven in the morning. What was everybody making so much noise about out in the hall?

"Shut up!" She threw her pillow at the door. It landed soundlessly. The clamor of voices continued. Shrieks, gasps—it sounded serious. Dahlia got out of bed, wrapped herself in her blanket, and went to see what was going on.

It seemed as if half the hall was congregated in front of the door to the triple at the end of the corridor. "Hey, some of us are still in dreamland," Dahlia called out to them. "What's the big news?"

She felt a half dozen pairs of startled eyes on her as she came down the hall. "You haven't

heard?" Gwen asked. "Where've you been hiding?"

"She got in late last night," Marion told
Gwen.

"What are you talking about?" Dahlia asked
as she walked toward the group. "Is somebody
going to tell me?" She noticed that Susan Kim,
Marion's roommate, was holding a copy of the
Register, the local newspaper. "What's going
on? Someone else get married?" she joked.

Susan held out the paper so Dahlia could
see. She pointed to the headline. *Attempted
Rape on Town Green. Attacker on the Loose.*

Dahlia let out a little gasp. "Can I see?" she
asked Susan. She scanned the article. "A student. A freshman. Phew, well, at least she's
okay, just a little bruised. But the guy got away?
God, it sounds awful. It's giving me the creeps
just reading about it. I wonder who she is." As
Dahlia looked up from the newspaper, she noticed that everybody's eyes were quickly shift-
ing to avoid hers. The whole group was silent.

"Hey, come on, guys. The paper said it was a
freshman. Do you know who it was?"

Marion nodded. "But—she wants it kept a
secret, Dahlia. You understand."

"So it's somebody we know?" Dahlia had a
horrible thought. Julie. She lived right next to

the Green. She felt herself start to shake. "Oh no, not Julie?"

"We'd better tell her, guys," Marion said. The others nodded.

"It was Sarah," Amanda said, teary-eyed.

"It's okay," Gwen said, as she took Amanda by the hand. "Sarah's going to be just fine. She needs some time to get over it, that's all."

"Apparently, a couple of people came to help when they heard her screaming, so she didn't get hurt or anything," Marion told her.

Dahlia felt a powerful mix of emotions—tremendous relief that Julie was okay and sadness for Sarah. "Where is she?" Dahlia asked.

"She left really early for breakfast. I don't think she slept at all. She was crying most of the night," Gwen said. "Her brother came and picked her up."

Her brother. Tim Pike. Dahlia still hurt, remembering the day he dumped her. That day was the beginning of Dahlia's misery on campus. But as much as she hated Tim for the way he treated her, it had nothing to do with Sarah. "I feel so bad for her," Dahlia said.

She could have sworn she saw a look of disbelief flash across Amanda's face. *Yeah, right,* she seemed to be saying. Since the thing with

125

Tim, Dahlia and Sarah hadn't exactly been best pals, and everyone knew it.

"I really do feel awful," Dahlia said again.

"We all do," Susan said.

"Shouldn't we do something for her?" Dahlia asked. No one, friend or otherwise, deserved what had happened to Sarah. But what could you do for somebody after they'd been attacked? You couldn't buy them presents to cheer them up. Besides, Dahlia doubted Sarah would want anything from her.

"I think she just wants everybody to respect her privacy," Marion said. "She wants to forget about it as fast as possible."

"I don't blame her," Dahlia said. She sighed. "Wow, what a welcome back, huh?" She was used to things like this happening in New York. But not in Madison, Ohio. "I can't believe it. And nobody has a clue about who did it?"

"Some sleazoid townie, probably," said Scott, running a hand through his long, blond hair.

"Probably," Amanda agreed.

"We were talking about organizing a buddy system," Susan said. "Until they find the guy."

"Yeah, if there's a maniac on the loose, who knows where he'll turn up next," Gwen said.

"Like no one walks alone after dark," Marion

said. "Hey, since you're alone, Dahlia, you can triple up with Susan and me."

"Thanks, guys." Marion might not be the coolest person around, but Dahlia could see that her offer was an act of real friendship. "Yeah, a buddy system sounds like a great idea," she said.

Bob stuck his skinny chest out and flexed an unimpressive muscle. "Feel free to call on me anytime, Dahlia. If you hear anything that goes bump in the night, just knock on my door."

"How the heck would you hear her, Bob?" Gwen injected. "You and Scott always have your stereo cranked so loud, the whole place could be invaded, and you wouldn't even know it." Her remark helped to break the tension.

"Hey, here comes your own personal security guard, Marion," Susan said, pointing down the hall at Fred Fryer. Dahlia noticed he was wearing the same outfit he had on a week ago when she'd last seen him getting on the bus to go home for break: plaid flannel shirt under a navy-blue parka, jeans, a Cincinnati Reds baseball cap, and brown loafers. Yep, he was perfect for Marion.

"Hi, everyone. Um, hi, Marion, how was your Thanksgiving?"

"Good. Lots of fun. We had turkey." Dahlia

could tell Marion was nervous seeing Fred for the first time since break.

"I—I thought that with all this stuff going on, you might want to walk to breakfast and then bio together."

"Sure, Fred. That's really nice of you," Marion said. She gave a jittery wave to Dahlia and the others. "See you guys. Be safe."

Dahlia watched the two of them walk down the hall. Marion immediately reached for Fred's hand, which she all but had to pry out of his pocket.

"Still no action, huh?" Dahlia asked. "That boy is so busy dissecting the birds and the bees, he forgets that he is one. Someone better tell him that Marion's not going to wait around forever."

"I'm working on Marion," Gwen said. "They'll be smooching by Christmas break."

"Well, at least we can count out one guy as the possible attacker," Bob said. "Fred wouldn't know what to do." He was the only one to laugh at his own sick joke.

Dahlia rolled her eyes. "That's hardly funny, Bob."

The campus snack bar was packed. In the line that formed at the long service counter, kids high-fived one another, and exchanged hugs and greetings after their vacation. Every booth and most of the tables were occupied. People streamed through the door glancing around to see who was there that they knew.

Julie, at a booth near the counter with Dahlia, was painfully aware of exactly who was town in here and who was gown. Kids pulling out their wallets to pay for coffee, fries, burgers, shakes—gown. Women flipping food on the grill, filling orders, manning the register—town. Julie watched a man in a custodian's uniform mopping up. He swirled the mop across the tiles toward a table of students lingering over their cups of coffee.

"Hey, can't you wait till we're out of here, pal?" one of the boys snapped as the man got too close to his sneakers.

The custodian scowled and pushed his mop right under the boy's table as if no one was there.

No respect, Julie thought. Not on either side. Was it getting worse? Probably not. It was probably just that Matt had gotten her noticing it more.

"Julie? Hey, wake up," Dahlia was saying. She reached across the table and shook Julie's arm.

"Huh? Oh, sorry."

"It's okay. I was saying how awful it must have been last night," Dahlia said. Julie had just finished telling Dahlia about her and Matt's part in the terrible event. "Wow, if you hadn't gotten there when you did . . ." She shook her head, her long, blond hair swirling around her shoulders.

"I know. But listen, Dahlia, don't say anything to Sarah about it, all right? I think she's heavily in the denial stage right now. Wants to pretend it never happened," Julie said.

"You don't have to worry about me," Dahlia said. "She doesn't really talk to me as it is."

"Oh, right." Not living in the dorm anymore, it sometimes slipped Julie's mind that Sarah and Dahlia were on the outs.

"I mean, I feel really bad for her and everything, but I don't think she'd be too into my trying to cheer her up, you know?"

"I guess," Julie said, dipping an onion ring in ketchup, then popping it into her mouth.

"Man, while that whole thing was happening, I was lying in bed thinking that I was actually glad to be back in dinky little Madison." Dahlia took a sip of coffee. "Now there's some nut running around out there."

"I know," Julie commiserated. She gave a little wave as a girl from her women's literature class went by. "Hey, Maggie!"

"Well, at least you've got Matt around the house to protect you," Dahlia commented. "The perfect husband."

Julie frowned. "Yeah, sure. He's out on his bike riding off the biggest fight we've ever had. Probably won't come back until he's hiked halfway around Lake Erie or something." Even though they had each apologized, the anger from their fight still lingered. Matt had barely spoken to her when they got up that morning.

"Sounds serious." Dahlia drained her coffee cup. "What happened?"

Julie shrugged. "We were both pretty upset about Sarah. I guess that's how it began. But then he started in on the same thing that's been bumming him out ever since he got out here. Town versus college. College versus town. He's got me obsessing now. Anyway, I'm not even sure how we got from Sarah to that, except that the whole town-gown thing's on Matt's mind in a major way."

"Mixed marriage, huh?" Dahlia said, injecting a note of levity into the conversation.

Julie gave a little laugh. "The thing is, living off campus, just Matt and me, and worrying about bills and all this grown-up stuff, I don't

131

feel very much like the typical college girl." She glanced around at the little groups of students in the snack bar. "I feel like I'm just pretending sometimes. Maybe that's part of why Matt and I are fighting."

Dahlia helped herself to one of Julie's onion rings. "Julie, you know what all these people in here are doing?"

Julie took a more careful look. A guy and a girl were kissing passionately in the corner booth, as if they were alone. A trio of girls, all in Madison sweatshirts, huddled together in a communal giggle. A bunch of jock guys darted glances at the girls.

"See those girls with their eyes glued to the door?" Dahlia went on. "The ones waiting to see who comes in here next?"

"Yeah?" Julie asked, following Dahlia's gaze to two girls in the booth next to the door. Both of them were sitting on the same side of the booth—the one with the view.

"Checking out the merchandise," Dahlia said. "They're all looking for romance, action. Maybe even for that 'special someone.'" She indicated the quotation marks by crooking two fingers on each hand. "Julie, plenty of your typical college kids, as you call them, would fly at the chance to trade places with you."

"I know," Julie said. "Still, sometimes I can't help feeling kind of envious of everyone coming back after vacation to their dorms and their dorm friends. I mean, if you have a fight with your roommate, there are plenty of other people to hang out with." She gave a feeble laugh.

"Well, all of us on the hall still think of you as one of us," Dahlia said. "And Matt—he's like an honorary member. Come on, every married couple fights. You've watched TV, haven't you? That's practically all they do. It's normal. It doesn't mean you two don't have something great going."

"You think?" But Dahlia wasn't there last night, when their voices were escalating in their little apartment, when Julie just wanted Matt to disappear. What would she have thought then?

"I'm sure. Hey, what do I have to do, tell you we're all totally jealous?" Dahlia said. "I believe in you guys. More than you know. So what if you fight once in a while? You love each other." Her eyes went briefly to the clock behind the food counter. "Well, listen, I should get to class. You're finished for the day?"

Julie nodded. All her classes met in the mornings, while Dahlia had made sure not to sign up for anything that started before eleven o'clock. "And that's if I skip breakfast," she'd said of her 11:00 A.M. psychology class.

Now Dahlia stood up and came around to Julie's side of the booth and leaned down to hug her. Julie rose to return the hug. "I missed you over vacation," Julie said.

"Ditto," Dahlia said. "I actually think I would have rather been hanging here."

"I don't know. That Tavern place sounds super-luxurious."

"Super-snooty," Dahlia corrected her. "Hey, take it easy, okay? And remember, Wilson Hall's still home if you get lonely."

"Thanks," Julie said. She watched Dahlia walk away, then stop to say something to a cute guy with dreadlocks and ripped jeans whom Julie had noticed around campus.

Julie bit into another onion ring. She wished she could believe Dahlia, but she felt less and less like one of the crowd. A half hour in the snack bar every once in a while was about the extent of her college hanging out. Now that she was married and lived off campus, the school had waived her campus dining requirements. She worked in the dining hall, but she didn't eat any of her meals there, didn't linger over dessert with her pals to put off going to the library for just another few minutes, no longer pretended to be reading in the study lounge at Wilson, knowing full well someone would come by and distract her. No more spontaneous dorm parties. By the time she found out about them, they were over.

Of course, where she didn't feel college enough, Matt seemed to feel she was too college. Julie remembered the sound of the bedroom door slamming the night before, like a single gunshot, closing her and Matt off from each other. She squeezed out some more ketchup. If Matt were in school, too, it would be so much easier. Well, in some ways. They'd also have an extra tuition to worry about then.

She looked over at the couple still locked at the lip. If only she'd met Matt here at Madison, like those two or—

"Julie!" Coming toward her, a grin on his fine-featured face, was Nick.

"Hey! Nick!" Julie stood up. They threw their arms around each other in a big hug. "Welcome back!" she said, her arms still around him. Nick was taller than Matt but thinner, his shoulders more angular under her hands.

"Missed you guys," Nick said as they released each other.

"I missed you." Julie slid back into the booth. There was something about having a reunion with him that made their friendship feel all the more real. "You got back okay."

"Yeah, I took the bus," Nick said. He sat down on the same side of the booth with her. "Got stuck next to this guy who wouldn't stop talking about everything he ate on Thanksgiving. If I had to hear about the sweet potato soufflé one more time . . ."

Julie laughed. Nick's blue-jeaned leg was touching hers. She was aware of his nearness, the amber streaks in his green eyes. "You should've pretended you were asleep," she said.

"Pretend? Who had to pretend?" Nick cracked. "Problem was, I don't think the guy noticed."

"Just hope he doesn't show up in one of your classes next semester," Julie said.

"With my luck he'll remember me from the bus ride and take a seat right next to me."

"Well, I just hope I don't wind up in that class, sitting on his other side."

"Really." Nick laughed. "Hey, it would be fun to have a class together. You and me, I mean."

"Yeah. Maybe next semester. What should we take?" Julie asked. She leaned in closer to him. To anyone who didn't know them, she thought, they looked like two regular college kids. Maybe even boyfriend and girlfriend.

Wait. What was she thinking? Nick was her friend—a real friend. And Matt's friend. Julie hoped that maybe he'd even be Dahlia's friend, if they could get over their bad start.

She shifted away from him just slightly. She was a married woman. A happily married woman, even if she and Matt had had a fight the night before. As Dahlia said, it happened to everybody.

Twelve

❧

"Not tonight, Jeff. I've really got to finish some reading." Dahlia paced her little room, phone receiver in hand. "Look, I'll see you later, okay?" Dahlia hung up the phone. *Blah!* Jeff, Mr. Super Macho from her theater class? Not if he were the last person left on the face of the earth.

She flopped down on her bed and went back to *The Scarlet Letter,* her English assignment for the week. She really could have used some company. But she wanted a friend, not Jeff. And not Charlie, who'd called earlier, or Franco, who lived two floors above her. Just hanging out with Julie, talking about life, or laughing about kids on campus and the college scene— that was what she wanted. Dahlia let out a sigh. She really missed Julie.

She felt like calling her. But what if Julie and Matt were in the middle of another marital squabble? Even worse, what if they were in the middle of making up and she interrupted them? No, it would be best to let Julie call her. If she did, they could go over to De-Caff, the campus coffee house, for Open Mike Comedy Night and De-Caff's freshly baked chocolate chip cookies. Uh-oh. Dahlia could feel a craving coming on. If it weren't for that maniac running loose, she wouldn't have wasted a second going over there by herself.

She got up and opened her door, then stuck her head out to look up and down the hall. Maybe someone else would want to go with her. But it was totally quiet. No voices coming from the triple. No Marion or Susan. Where were Bob and Scott tonight? It wasn't often that there wasn't a rock concert pouring out of their room.

Dahlia frowned. Warm cookies, the bittersweet chips still half melted. She could make a run for it. She hesitated a moment, then reached for her coat on the hook by the door. After all, she was a New Yorker. If she could survive eighteen years there, what were the chances of anything happening here? She'd go quickly and make sure no one was following her. And just in case, she'd keep her room key in her hand. She'd read somewhere that in case of an emergency, it could be a very handy self-defense weapon.

But as she stepped into the chilly night and headed across campus, Dahlia felt more vulnerable on the near-empty walkway that cut across North Campus than she did in Manhattan. There might have been thousands of loonies in the Big Apple, but at least there were bright lights in the big city. Now, with a haunting moonless black sky overhead, and only a few sporadically spaced lamplights, she felt like a spooked heroine in one of those awful slasher movies. *Madman in Madison, Part Two.* Dahlia felt her pace quickening with each step she took toward the café. She found herself running the last fifty or so steps to De-Caff's entrance in the basement of South Hall.

She breathed a sigh of relief as she pushed open the door and was hit with a blast of warmth and the aroma of brewing coffee and freshly baked cookies. At a dozen or so little round tables, each one lit by a single, glowing candle, students sat over steaming mugs. The low ceiling made the place seem even cozier. Up front, there was a makeshift stage lit by a single theater lamp. The whole atmosphere seemed like a step back in time. Dahlia had seen places like this in hippie movies and in a few old photos of her mom and dad when they were in their "groovy" phase—the one that probably lasted about ten minutes.

Dahlia headed for the cookies and coffee, getting in line behind three other people. Onstage, a chubby-faced black girl stood at the mike.

"Anybody seen the latest in PC fashions? My ecology prof, Mr. Stay-Green, decided he'd give Calvin Klein a run for his money. He's designed a whole line of pants, dresses, socks, and underwear made entirely of plants and veggies. My fave are the lettuce-leaf bras and the spinach panties. The new line is due out in May, but with a spring frost, it may not be ready till late summer." A hearty round of laughter kept the comedienne's spirits riding high. "Just in case, he's working on an alternative. You know radical eco professors—always looking for an alternative. Thank you, you've been great." She smiled and took a bow as everybody applauded. Dahlia laughed, happy she hadn't let her fears keep her away.

Her laughter stopped abruptly, though, as her gaze settled on Nick, sitting at a front table with a few other guys. Dahlia felt herself instantly torn between trying to get his attention and pretending she didn't see him at all. But, as if feeling her gaze on him, he turned toward her, caught her eye, and gave a stiff little wave. She could sense the awkwardness left over from their misadventure coloring his expression. Dahlia smiled tentatively and waved back. *Why does he have to be so cute?* she wondered.

"Can I help you?" the girl behind the coffee bar asked, interrupting Dahlia's preoccupation with Nick. "Mocha Java or decaf house blend tonight."

"A mug of the Mocha Java and a cookie, please," Dahlia said. "Um, better make that two cookies." They were oversize, and stuffed with chips and walnuts, but she'd been known to eat a half dozen or so in one sitting.

As the girl put the cookies on a plate, Dahlia could taste them already. "That'll be two seventy-five, please."

Dahlia reached into her coat pocket and fished for her wallet. But it wasn't there. She tried her jeans pockets, hoping to find a loose bill or two. "Oops, I think I left my money back at the dorm," she said, flustered. She checked her coat again. "I guess I spaced out. I'm really sorry. Can I bring it tomorrow?" She'd been so worried about that psycho that she hadn't even thought about taking her wallet.

"Hey, Bill? She left her money back at her dorm," the girl behind the bar called over to a ponytailed guy who was adjusting the microphone onstage. Everyone in the room seemed to turn around at once.

But before the guy was even off the stage, Dahlia saw Nick stand up and make his way across the room toward her. He was digging his hand into his pocket and pulling out his wallet. "I'll get it," he said, coming up beside Dahlia.

Dahlia felt a wave of surprise. "Thanks a lot, Nick." Maybe she'd misinterpreted his greeting.

Nick shrugged. "No biggie. I owe you." There was an uncomfortable silence. "So, I guess you made it back okay. I mean, they fixed your car and all?"

Dahlia let out a little laugh. "Yeah, they fixed it. A couple of fuses and some wiring problem. The mechanic was terrific. Fifty bucks covered the whole thing."

"Great," Nick said.

He seemed a bit anxious. He looked at his watch. "Well, I guess I'll see you around, Dahlia." He started to go.

"Hey, you sure you don't want to stay and have a cookie with me? I mean, you paid for it and all. Besides, I think I might have over-ordered a little," Dahlia said.

"Uh . . ." Nick seemed to freeze up. *Same old story,* Dahlia figured. *Doesn't want to be seen with the spoiled rich kid.* "Nah. I was just telling my pals I had to head back to the dorm to hit the books."

Right. At eleven-thirty at night, he was about to start studying. "Sure. Whatever," Dahlia said flatly. She sat down at the nearest empty table.

Nick took a step away, then turned back. "Oh, Dahlia?"

"Yeah?"

"Listen, have you seen Julie since what happened on the Green?"

"Julie?" Dahlia nodded. Suddenly Nick was coming back over and sitting down across from her. *Well, the secret password,* she thought.

Onstage, the guy with the ponytail blew into the microphone. "Testing. One-two-three-hello? All right! And now, to keep you howling, the one and only Michael David Bunson. This guy's a scream. Ahhhhhh!"

Dahlia groaned. "Oh, brother. Bunson's in my theater class. This could be terrible." She took a bite of her cookie. "Mmmm, this is great. Sure you don't want one?"

Nick shook his head. "So you think she's okay?"

"Huh? Oh, Julie. Yeah, well, she's upset about the attack, but she'll deal."

"Yeah. I saw her for a minute the other day," Nick said. "She seemed pretty shaken up about it."

Michael David Bunson came onstage wearing a Madison sweatshirt. He also had on a pair of greasy, ripped black jeans. He held a bottle of spring water in one hand and a beer bottle in the other. "I'm the Town-Gown Kid," he announced to a howling audience.

Dahlia didn't think it was so funny. She noticed that Nick wasn't laughing either.

"Hey, I was just reading in the paper," Bunson began, "about how the town is thinking about closing down the high school. Not enough of an enrollment. Maybe they should just make the tests a little easier. Like instead of giving four multiple-choice possibilities, they should just give one. That way there's a little better chance some of them'll pass, don't you think?"

"Oh, brother. I'll bet he bought that joke

from some desperate joke salesman," Nick said.

"Dumb," Dahlia agreed, a little embarrassed for the guy.

But Michael David Bunson was getting lots of laughs. The all-student audience was eating it up. "What's the difference between a townie and a college student? Everything." Laughter. "What's a townie without a beer in his hand? Asleep." The laughter continued.

Dahlia understood why. There was so much town-gown tension even before the attack. Now people were scared, too. And they needed an outlet. But she thought the comic was way out of line.

"How many townies does it take to screw in a light bulb?" he continued. "Two. One to screw it in, and the other to hold his beer while he's screwing it. Why did the townie cross the road?" The audience quieted to a whisper. " 'Cause there was a pretty freshman girl on the other side."

A couple of dry laughs, but mostly loud hoots and boos, followed. Someone shouted at him to shut up. Nick seconded the request, standing up and yelling, "Enough!"

"I think I've had enough, too," Dahlia said.

"Yeah. Look, since you're alone, I guess I

really ought to walk you back to your dorm. With everything that's going on, and stuff . . ." But Nick didn't sound overly excited about it.

"It's okay, Nick. I'm a big girl." Dahlia wasn't looking forward to another scary sprint back across campus, but her dorm was out of Nick's way, and she had her pride.

"It's no big deal, really. I'll walk you back and hit the books after. Really, I insist. Julie wouldn't want me letting her good friend walk around alone at night after what happened."

Julie again. Boy, Nick sure was the perfect friend—so long as your name was Julie Miller. They left De-Caff, side by side, but Dahlia felt sure they were still miles apart.

Thirteen

❧

Julie felt like a celebrity.

"Julie, hi!" said a tall, skinny girl from her women's lit class. "Saw your piece in the *Register* today. Way to go!"

"Yeah, tell it like it is," said the girl's companion.

"Thanks," Julie said, flashing them both a huge smile. Suddenly it seemed as if everyone on campus knew who she was. The local newspaper had called her only a few days earlier to let her know they'd decided to run her article. They wanted to check the facts and go over a few points with her, and to let her know she wouldn't be getting paid. Julie didn't mind. All the recognition was making her feel great.

"Saw your article," said a tall, husky boy she recognized from working at the dining hall. *Ex-*

tra gravy on the meat loaf, was the way Julie thought of him. She didn't know his name, but apparently, he knew hers. "Julie, right? Yeah, saw your article." Julie wasn't sure if that meant he liked it or hated it, but he'd certainly noticed it—and her.

"Julie! Hey, Julie, wait up!" she heard a girl's voice calling out to her a few moments later. She turned around to see Marion hurrying toward her, a red hat with a pom-pom bouncing crazily on top of her head.

"Julie, you're famous!" Marion crowed as she caught up with her.

Julie laughed. She *did* feel like a real Madison Madwoman today. Which was awfully nice after feeling so left out lately.

"I think it was great the way you stuck up for Sar—oops!" Marion clapped a hand over her mouth. "I know no one's supposed to know she was the one, but—"

"But it's a small school," Julie finished for her.

"Yeah. I guess a lot of people know. I feel so terrible for her," Marion said, her voice dropping to a whisper, even though there was no one else near enough to hear them. "I mean, I start to forget all about it, and then I see her in the study lounge or the bathroom, or some-

149

where, and I think how awful it must have been. . . ."

Julie nodded, wondering, for a moment, if all the attention she was getting was wrong, grounded as it was in Sarah's bad luck. She had a flash of Sarah, lying on the ground, her clothes disheveled, terror in her eyes.

Still, Julie and Matt had saved Sarah from something even worse, and she'd done her best to support Sarah with the article the *Register* had just printed. She and Marion walked in silence for a few minutes. A strong wind was blowing up around them.

"Well, I'm going this way," Julie finally said, pointing toward Fischer Hall, one of the main classroom buildings.

"Oh. I told Fred I'd meet him in the bio lab," Marion said, her voice turning dreamy.

Julie smiled. "Secret moments in science?" She wondered whether Marion and Fred had kissed yet. Poor Marion. It had become something of a joke among the students on her hall.

Whatever the situation, Marion looked happily embarrassed. "We have to finish working on Mort."

"Mort?"

"The fetal pig we're dissecting."

150

Julie made a face. "Well, if that's your idea of fun . . ." she said, laughing.

Marion laughed, too. "Yeah, well . . . see you, Julie. And congratulations again. I'm going to cut your article out and save it. It's really neat knowing a published writer."

"Thanks, Marion." Julie turned and headed over to Fischer. As she approached the low, modern building, with its tall, narrow, finger-like windows, she spotted Nick, about to enter the building. She broke into a light jog and caught up with him just inside the front doors.

"Hey, Nick!" She tugged lightly at the sleeve of his parka.

He turned around. "Hey! Our campus star!" His cheeks were pink from the wind. He leaned down and gave Julie a little hug. She felt a tingle. "I liked what you wrote," he said, straightening back up. "It made a lot of sense."

"Thanks. I just said what I felt."

"Yeah, well, not everyone can say it so well," Nick complimented her. "Oh, listen, I tried to call you guys yesterday. When you see Matt, tell him I'm psyched to go for a bike ride on his day off."

Julie nodded. "Sure. I know he'll be psyched, too. He was saying he needed some real exercise. Just going from table to table and mopping floors isn't cutting it. Catch you later, Nick."

"Definitely. See you, Julie."

Julie sailed into journalism flush with Nick's praise—and the warmth of the hug she could still feel.

"Ah, the woman with the voice!" Professor Copeland announced as soon as she'd come through the door. "Our woman who speaks for all other women."

Julie faced him, intent on holding on to her confident mood. "You read my article, sir."

"I did, Ms. Miller." Usual overemphasis on the "Ms." Wouldn't Copeland ever get used to it? "And I'd like to begin class with a question," he continued. "Not just to Ms. Miller, but to all of you. I'm interested in finding out what the difference is between expressing your emotions—spilling your guts, as you might call it—and writing an op-ed article."

Julie held in a groan as she slipped into a seat near the door. Why did he always have to be so hard on her? It would be so nice if once, just once, Copeland tried encouraging her instead of humiliating her.

"It's the same thing," called out John Graham, his long, red hair pulled back in a ponytail that morning. "An op-ed says how you feel about an issue in the news."

"Mr. Graham, I'd prefer it if you didn't call out," Professor Copeland said. "Especially when you don't have something more enlightening to add to the discussion. There are some rather important things that separate an op-ed from an emotional outburst."

Emotional outburst, Julie thought. *Thanks a lot.* She'd believed she'd done a pretty good piece of writing. And so had plenty of other people she'd run into that morning.

She felt herself stiffen as Professor Copeland picked up a piece of chalk. You never knew if he was going to lance it out into the classroom like a missile or put it to a more traditional purpose. His lip was curled in faint disgust. "Anyone? No other answers?" He turned to the board and wrote, "Op-ed—airing your _____."

Opinion, Julie thought. But like everyone else in the class, she was afraid to say it. You never knew when Copeland had a trick up his sleeve.

"I'm waiting. Miss McQuade?"

"Point of view? Opinion?" Megan McQuade said nervously from the back of the room.

"Very good, Ms. McQuade," Professor Copeland said, sarcasm dripping from his words.

"Airing your opinion. That doesn't mean jumping to conclusions. That doesn't mean making accusations that you can't support. That doesn't mean stating your opinions as fact."

Julie slumped down in her seat. That was the problem with having a voice. It meant people like Copeland picked on you.

The professor walked toward the back of the room, his step heavy for such a little man. He stopped directly in front of Julie. "Aren't you making some assumptions, Ms. Miller, that you oughtn't to make? Implying something that could be wrong? Are you saying the man in the restaurant is the assailant?"

Julie looked down at her desktop. "I'm saying no one knows," she mumbled. "But that what the guy said is, in itself, enough of an attack against women. That was my point, sir." *It's a woman thing, you wouldn't understand,* she thought.

"And so he's guilty of the attack? Because he said something you disagree with?"

"I didn't say that at all. I just said the guy was wrong. He was wrong for what he said. And whoever attacked—the girl—was wrong, too."

Julie let Copeland go on, storming back to the blackboard and underlining and re-underlining the phrases he'd written. Three months into the semester, she was almost getting used to what seemed like his mission to humiliate her. Almost getting used to it, but not quite.

She thought about the first time Copeland had brought her to the brink of tears on her first day of class. Back on that September morning, Julie had rushed out of class and raced to call Matt. Four hundred miles away in Philadelphia, he'd still been able to cheer her up, make her feel that Copeland wasn't worth crying over.

This time she could have a real hug and kiss to make her feel better. Live and in person. Matt would tell her that Copeland was a little man with a big ego. And then she could go back to being a celebrity for a day.

As soon as Julie finished working the lunch shift at the dining hall, she threw her apron into the laundry bin in the back room and beat a quick exit out the kitchen door. She walked briskly in the cold afternoon but took the long way, skirting the town green and the site of the incident.

All the attention she received had been flattering at first, but as the day wore on, she began wishing that someone, anyone, would talk to her about something else. She couldn't wait to get home and forget, for just a few hours, about what had happened to Sarah Pike. She'd wanted to speak out, make her feelings known, but she hadn't counted on how hard it was to be reminded over and over of the awful moment she and Matt had found Sarah.

The worst part was that some of the things people were saying were making Julie wonder if she'd done the right thing by airing her feelings in the *Register*.

"If that girl had wanted everyone talking about her, she'd have said something herself," a girl with dark, flashing eyes had told Julie as she'd pushed her lunch tray along the service line.

"She thinks any guy who says something about some girl is going to go out there and attack her," Julie had overheard a boy in the mailroom saying earlier.

Of course, most of the campus was behind her. And all the attention was exciting. But Professor Copeland hadn't been the only one to criticize her. Julie sighed, walking past Books and Things without even pausing to see what was displayed in the window. All she wanted was to be in the privacy of her home: have a long, hot bath and an even longer snuggle with Matt.

She took a brief look inside Secondhand Rose, the thrift shop beneath their apartment, before heading toward the door. As she climbed the stairs, she heard voices coming from inside the apartment. *Oh, no! Visitors.* Usually, Julie looked forward to her friends' stopping by. It made her feel a little less like she'd left the dorm life behind. But right now, she was in no mood for company.

She took her keys out of the zip pocket of her canvas shoulder bag. They jangled against each other. "I don't want to name names," she heard Matt saying angrily, as she fit the key in the lock and opened their front door.

The two policemen from the night of the attack were in the living room. The younger one sat in the leopard-print armchair. The older one stood in the middle of the room, with Matt facing him, arms crossed. As she stepped inside, all three of them turned to look at Julie.

"What I told my wife was confidential," Matt said to the policemen, but his eyes were on her, holding her in a bitter gaze. He gave the word *wife* an unpleasant emphasis. Julie felt herself tighten up inside. "I had no idea she was planning on publishing what I told her for the whole town to read."

Julie managed a few numb steps toward him.

She couldn't believe what Matt was saying. So much for his being proud of her article.

"Is it Carl Sever?" the younger officer asked. Matt was silent.

"We've already been checking around. We know Carl Sever spends a lot of time in the Barn and Grill. And he fits your description of the assailant. We just need your confirmation."

"What description?" Matt asked. "All I saw was his back!"

"Carl's the one who was making all the noise in the restaurant, wasn't he?"

"We just want to ask him a few questions," the older one added. "No one's going to get locked up if they didn't do anything, son. We just need your cooperation, that's all."

Julie thought about the terror in Sarah's eyes that night. Now her terror might have a name. Carl Sever. "Matt, why won't you tell them?" she said. Her anger vibrated in her words.

"Fine!" Matt shouted. "If that's what you want. A name. Carl Sever. He's the one who was shooting off his mouth. And that's *all* he did!"

"Thank you. Both of you," the senior officer said. "Well, I guess that does it."

"Ma'am," the younger one echoed, touching the brim of his cap. "We owe you a big thank-you."

As soon as they were gone, Matt hit the ceiling. "And what if he's not the guy who attacked Sarah?" he yelled at Julie. "What if he's innocent? You believe those cops about not hauling him in? What if they arrest him, just because your whole school is out for town blood?"

Julie clenched her fists at her side. "And what if he *is* the one, Matt?" *Sarah: her shirt pushed up, her skin bare to the cold, her dirty arms, her face filled with fear.* "What if he almost raped Sarah? And he's out there. Free."

"What makes you so sure? Because he's some crass townie?" Matt shot back.

Julie could feel the hot sting of tears. No, she wasn't sure. She wasn't sure of anything. Not whether that awful Carl guy was the one who'd attacked Sarah or whether she should have written her article—she wasn't even sure about Matt. How could she be sharing her life with someone who cared more about some drunk creep than about one of her friends? "What's so awful about getting that Carl guy to answer some questions? If you're so certain he's innocent, why would he mind?"

Matt shook his head, a look of disgust on his

face. "Sometimes you are just so naive. How would you feel if a couple of cops came and dragged you out of your house and accused you of some horrible crime that you didn't commit? And it's going to be *my* fault. Because I thought I could trust you. Next thing I know, without even a peep out of you to warn me, what I told you in private is blasted all over the newspaper."

"So I should just shut up. Like Sarah. Is that what you're saying? Gee, that's a really great way to fight this kind of thing."

"Julie, I want to nail the guy as much as you do. I'm just saying you shouldn't go accusing people without any evidence."

"Evidence?" Matt was starting to sound like Professor Copeland. "What evidence? Another victim? Only this time, no one's around to stop the guy?" Julie brushed past Matt and stormed into the bedroom. She slammed the door. Let him sleep in the armchair tonight.

She threw herself diagonally onto their bed. It was only this morning that Nick had called her the campus star and made her feel so confident about what she'd had published in the *Register*. Now she almost wished she'd never written a word. She tried to call up the reassuring sensation of Nick's praise—and his hug, the way he'd held her for a moment. She squeezed her eyes closed and reached for the image. But there were too many bad feelings in the way.

Fourteen

❧

What if she'd been wrong to write that article? Julie felt a prickle of doubt as she made her way down her old hall. Maybe she never should have sent her piece to the *Register*. She stopped in front of the triple at the end of the hall and gave a tentative knock.

"Yeah?" said a voice inside. It sounded like Sarah.

"It's me. Julie."

There was a squeak like a chair being pushed back. Then the shuffle of feet. The door opened. "Hi," Sarah said noncommittally. She didn't ask Julie in.

Julie tried to read the look in Sarah's blue eyes, but they were studiously blank. "I—um—came to see how you were doing," she explained.

"Oh. Thanks. I'm okay. I'm fine," Sarah answered tonelessly.

"Sarah?" a male voice said from inside the room. There was another set of footsteps, and Sarah's brother, Tim, appeared behind her in the doorway, blond, handsome, and imposing in size. He put a protective hand on his sister's shoulder. Tim was a halfback for the Madison Madmen; no one was going to mess with Sarah while he was around.

"Hi, Tim," Julie said. She was glad Tim was there for his sister, but she'd never felt comfortable around him. Not after the way he'd used Dahlia and then dumped her. And now she felt even more uncomfortable because Sarah was so distant.

Julie remembered cradling Sarah in her arms on the Green, holding her hand in the police car on the way home, sitting with her—right here in the dorm—until she was ready to try to sleep. Now Julie felt like an unwanted guest. She looked back at Sarah. "You're mad about what I wrote."

Sarah studied her feet.

"She just doesn't want to be reminded," Tim answered for her. "And now everybody's talking about it even more."

"Look," Sarah said, not meeting Julie's gaze.

"I'm not mad. I'm—upset. Not with you. With the whole thing. It's like Tim says. I want to put it behind me."

Julie nodded slowly, but she didn't think Sarah was going to be able to put anything behind her by pretending that it had never happened. "Sarah, if you feel like talking, come over any time."

She turned to leave. She couldn't help feeling low. There was a growing list of people who were decidedly not excited about seeing her words in print—and Sarah agreed with them. Sarah—the person who counted most in all of this. Sarah plainly wished Julie had never written that article. Ditto Matt. Could both of them be wrong? Julie heard Sarah's door close. Once again, she was afraid that she'd made a mistake. A big one, involving people's deepest feelings.

And Julie couldn't even talk to Matt about it. She couldn't talk to him about anything these days without having it turn into a battle. She walked down the hall. Maybe she *had* been too quick to jump to conclusions about that guy Carl. But Matt was too quick to defend him, just because he was from town. College kids, townies—how had this happened? And how had Julie and Matt let it tear them apart? Back in Philadelphia, they'd been a team. Once upon a time it felt as if they could have taken on the world together.

Almost automatically, Julie stopped in front of her old room and knocked on the door. No answer. She tried the handle, but the door was locked. She picked up the purple Magic Marker attached to the message board with an elastic cord. "D. Sorry I missed you. Come by if you want. J."

She stood there for a moment longer. During the short time she'd lived in this dorm, she'd missed Matt so much, she didn't think she could live without him. Maybe she'd been wrong. Maybe it would have been better if she was still single and living in Room 103, Wilson, with Dahlia.

"Hey, wait up!" Matt heard Nick shouting from behind. Matt braked to a stop. His mountain bike skidded a few feet along the hard dirt path by the river. He turned around to see Leon "the Lip" turning the bend, and a few seconds later, Nick appeared, pedaling and panting furiously. Matt had been riding hard for nearly an hour, but there was so much anger and frustration bottled up inside him, he felt as if he could keep going all day.

As Nick and Leon pulled up next to Matt, Nick raised his arms in the air. "I confess. I'm a wimp. Too many hours in the library getting soft," he said between huge gasps for air. "You should have warned me that I'd be riding with an Olympic contender."

"I don't know about you, but I'm taking the train back," Leon said as he got off his bike and collapsed on the ground by the edge of the stream.

"I'm with you." Nick got off and flopped down next to Leon. "Matt, I thought you said this was a shortcut to the quarry."

"No comment," Leon said, still struggling to catch his breath. "Hey, Matt. You going to join us for a rest? Five minutes, okay?"

Matt got off his bike and sat down between his friends, although he would rather have kept on riding as fast as possible. Exercise was the best medicine he knew of when things were bad. And things were real bad. "Okay. Five minutes."

"Well, what do you know, the guy speaks. Three words, but it's a start," Nick said.

"Yeah, Matt, what's with you, man? I thought I was the one who played the blues." Leon laughed. "What's bugging you, anyway?"

Matt shrugged. "Start with Julie and end

with Carl and the Barn and Grill. And everything in between." He picked up a pebble and hurled it into the water. "Julie writes that article, the cops come looking for their man, then I find out Carl's split town, and then—"

"Carl split town? Since when?" Leon asked, sounding surprised.

"All I heard is that when the cops came looking for him, he'd left already. He's gone, with no forwarding address. And I don't blame him at all. I mean, you think he'd get a fair trial in this town? No way."

"Hey, slow down, Matt," Nick said. "I plead ignorant. Maybe I've missed something hitting the books all the time, but who's this guy Carl?"

Matt gave a sharp laugh. "That all depends on who you ask. I think he's just a guy from town who got too drunk one night and shot off his mouth. But according to Julie, the police, and practically everybody on campus, he's the guy who attacked the college student."

"You mean the guy Julie mentioned in the article she wrote?" Nick asked.

"Yeah, that's right. Carl Sever. The guy she and everybody else are trying to pin this thing on."

"Yo, easy, Matt. Now I understand why you've been pedaling that bike like such a maniac," Leon said. "But I was in the Barn and Grill that night, too, remember? Carl was out of line, man. If he split town, it might be for the obvious reason that he's got something to hide."

"And it might be because he's not interested in an encounter with the college-approved, Madison, Ohio, lynching squad. Innocent before being proven guilty doesn't mean anything around here," Matt said, pounding his fist on the hard ground. "And Julie's article didn't do a thing for anybody. Now the students and townies are more divided than ever. They hate each other. I go to work, and since I'm married to Julie, I get treated like Benedict Arnold."

"Hey, Matt," Nick said. "Maybe I'm wrong, but don't you think you read too much into Julie's article? I don't recall there being so much emphasis on the town-gown thing. Julie just pointed out a problem that a lot of us refuse to admit exists," Nick pointed out. "The article was mostly about women on campus being afraid to speak out when they do feel threatened—by any man, not just someone from town. A lot of people think Julie's article was pretty important."

"A lot of college people, you mean."

"I'm not a college people," Leon said. "And I

think she made a lot of sense. And as for the town-gown thing, it's not like it's anything new around here. I've lived in Madison all my life, Matt. The tension between the two groups is sort of like the weather. One day it's bad, the next day it's not so bad, and the next day it's bad again. It's always been like that, and it always will be."

"So now you guys are ganging up on me." Matt couldn't believe he was getting it from his friends, too. "Look, I'll admit it. Carl's not the most upstanding guy. Fact is, what he said the other night really got me bent out of shape. But the real issue isn't whether it was Carl or not. Or whether Julie's article was on the money or not. She betrayed my confidence. I didn't tell her about Carl's comments so she could blab it all over the world."

"Maybe not, but if Julie didn't, somebody else would have," Leon said. "There were a lot of people in the restaurant that night. Someone would have gotten the word out on Carl."

"I suppose." Matt dug his fingers into the dirt.

The flow of the stream, the smell of the crisp, clean earth reminded Matt of the backwoods near his house in Philly, where he and his friend Steven had spent so much time riding bikes and hiking. He missed being there. He hated to admit it, even to himself, but ever since he and Julie had started fighting, he'd had more than a few moments of wanting to go home. He picked up another stone and threw it into the water. It split in half as it smashed against a rock.

"So . . . I talked to my dad last night. I called him from the Barn and Grill right after I got a heavy dose of the cold-shoulder treatment from a few of the regulars. He offered me my old job back at the Fast Lane."

Nick straightened up and arched an eyebrow. "It's not the first time he's done that, right? You told me he asks you to come back every time you talk with him. You wouldn't really do it, would you?" he asked. There was a note of surprise and deep concern in his voice.

"I don't know." Matt shrugged. "It's so hard living with someone. It seems as if Julie and I fight more than we have fun these days. We don't even like the same toothpaste. She says I snore, and I think she hogs the bed." He picked up another stone and tossed it. "If I went back to Philly, I could be manager of the whole place again. Me, manager of the most popular club in

Philadelphia. And with business hopping, we could open up a second club. I could have my own club before I turned twenty! Not like here, where I'm part-time waiter, full-time busboy and dishwasher."

"I can't believe what I'm hearing," Nick said. "And what about Julie? I thought you married her because you loved her. Didn't you guys make a lifelong commitment? How did it go? 'For richer or poorer, for better or worse'? "

Nick's words stung. Richer or poorer? They could barely pay the bills. Better or worse? Today things were definitely worse. Lifelong commitment? Matt's parents had made that same commitment. The stinging memory of his mother walking out of the house a dozen years ago, when Matt was seven, was suddenly as fresh in his head as if it had happened yesterday. Matt hadn't seen her since, and didn't want to, either. "I don't know anything anymore," Matt confessed.

"You're talking crazy, man. You'd leave Julie, just like that? But she's the best and you know it!" Leon said.

"Yeah, you'd better do some serious thinking, Matt," Nick warned. "Julie's way too special to give up."

Matt needed another stone. Something to throw. Anything to release his tension.

"Well, I'm all rested up," Leon said, his voice full of pretend enthusiasm.

"Me, too." Nick got up. "Let's ride some more, what do you say?"

"Sure." Matt got up, too. He'd said enough and heard enough. Maybe another few hours on the bike would help clear his head.

"Did you do under the sofa?" Julie shouted above the sound of the vacuum cleaner. She paused, dust rag in hand, to watch Matt.

Matt threw her a dirty look. "Guess what, Julie?" he yelled back. "I can vacuum just fine without any help, thank you. Or did they teach you some extra-fancy vacuuming techniques at college?"

Julie frowned. "You don't have to be so snotty. I was just asking."

"And I was just answering."

Julie blew out a breath and went over and turned off the vacuum cleaner. "You know, you really make me feel guilty about going to school. If you think I ought to quit and get a full-time job, at least be honest enough to come right out and say it."

Matt studied the rug. "Look, I'm sorry,

okay? I didn't mean it. Really." He let out an abbreviated laugh. "And maybe I *wasn't* getting under the sofa. I didn't mean to get on your case. Promise."

Julie shrugged. "I guess we're both pretty on edge these days. I shouldn't have been supervising your vacuuming job—I suppose I skip under the sofa, too."

Matt grinned. "Then I really better get under there. Could be some nasty stuff hiding out." He turned the vacuum cleaner back on.

But a few minutes later he turned it off again. "Listen, maybe we need to have a little fun instead of cleaning the apartment. Get out of here for a while."

Julie stopped dusting the bookshelves and looked at him. "I hear an idea percolating," she said. "Or are you just trying to get out of the housework?"

"Both." Matt laughed. "Leon told me about this funky old diner out by the lake. It's in one of those Silver Bullets—you know, those really cool old trailers? Anyway, it's supposed to have great food—homemade soups and stuff. We could go there for lunch."

Julie hesitated. She had a ton of schoolwork to do, the house was a pigsty, and it was her turn to do the grocery shopping. On the other hand, getting out of Madison for a few hours sounded awfully tempting—getting out and being Julie who loved Matt, and not Julie-hyphen-wife, or Julie-hyphen-student. Getting out and just having it be the way it used to be with Matt.

She tossed the dust rag into the kitchen sink. "Twist my arm," she joked. "I'll get my coat."

A few minutes later, they were both bundled up and riding down Main Street on Matt's motorcycle. Julie wrapped her arms around Matt's waist. "You think they'll have homemade pie à la mode?" she yelled, lifting the visor on her helmet so Matt could hear her.

"All kinds," Matt yelled back.

Julie grinned, feeling the rush of cold wind as they sped forward. A half a block up, she could see the stoplight at the corner turning amber. Matt squeezed the brakes. As they slowed down, an ear-shattering, metallic squeal split the air.

Julie grimaced. "What was that?"

"Brakes," Matt said. "I really need to get some new ones before these wear down completely." He came to a complete stop at the light.

"Isn't it dangerous to be riding around with them like this?"

Matt shrugged.

Julie felt a flutter of nervousness. "Maybe we shouldn't take such a long ride."

"I've been riding with them like this for weeks," Matt said with a trace of irritation.

"And you haven't done anything about it?"

Julie felt Matt go tight. "I thought we were going to have some fun for once."

For once. The way Matt said it made it sound as if it was her fault. "We could go somewhere closer."

"Like the Rath?" Matt said sourly. You had to have a college ID to set foot in the campus pub. "I thought we were out of here."

"You know, it's not like I don't want to go, too," Julie said. "I just want us to be safe. You can understand that, can't you?"

Matt blew out a breath. "Yeah, I guess you're right."

"And fix the brakes, okay? I sort of care a little bit about what happens to you," Julie added, her tone lighter.

"I sort of care what happens to you, too," Matt said. He made a U-turn and headed back up Main Street. "Maybe we should just go for a walk around town."

Julie agreed. She took his hand after they'd gotten off his bike and removed their helmets. But the promise of the afternoon was gone, and they both knew it.

Fifteen

❧

"Huh? You want more macaroni and cheese?" Julie tried to focus on her job. "Yeah, sure." She scooped a portion of the orange, pasty noodles from the steaming metal container onto a half dozen or so small serving plates and put them up on one of the glass service shelves.

She made a quick survey to see what else was running low. *Okay on lima beans and beets. Need more carrots.* She filled several more tiny, white ceramic bowls with quarter-sized slices of overdone carrots. How could she concentrate on soggy vegetables when her life with Matt was such a mess? On the other hand, she couldn't afford not to concentrate. She needed this job—and all the extra shifts her boss, Mr. Raymond, could give her. It wasn't exactly a job for a rocket scientist, but the rent was due soon, and then there were the brakes on Matt's motorcycle.

Julie watched the line of students pushing their trays along. There was that girl who ate only white foods for the first part of the year. Since Thanksgiving, she'd switched to brown. Meat loaf, peanut butter on wheat bread, Coke, chocolate pudding. And here came the guy with the incredible collection of baseball caps, helping himself to a dish of lima beans. Today he had on a black and orange San Francisco Giants cap.

Julie frowned. Sometimes she felt so envious —imagining that some of her fellow Madmen and -women didn't have anything more to worry about than what to choose for dinner or which hat to wear to the dining hall. Maybe that wasn't exactly true. Everyone did have his or her own problems. Some of them had big ones, like Sarah's. Or smaller problems, like struggling to pass a tough course or breaking up with a boyfriend.

Still, it seemed so easy to be a normal college student. Someone who could spend some of the money from a school job on a new pair of earrings once in a while, or a meal out. Someone who didn't have to go home every night and fight with her husband. Someone who could still rely on Mom and Dad to help out when things got rough.

Julie felt a wave of unhappiness at the thought of her parents. She was angry at them, but she missed them, too. Before Matt had come out, she'd been in touch with them regularly by mail and phone. Then, suddenly, the big freeze. She wondered what her family was doing right then. Probably sitting down to dinner around the kitchen table, her father saying a prayer while Tommy hungrily eyed his roast beef.

Julie smiled a bittersweet smile as she thought of Tommy. She'd sent him a postcard a few days ago of the corner of Main and Center, on the bottom of which she'd written, "Love from the big city." Thanksgiving had been the last time she'd heard his voice. It had been only a week and a half ago, but it seemed longer. Much longer.

Julie was afraid she might start crying right in the middle of work. As silly as it was, she wished she could be about six years old right then—when boys were people you caught frogs with down at the pond, and parents were, well, parents. Grown-ups, adults, who you were sure would be there to take care of you forever. Six years old. Back when Mary Beth was eight, and it seemed as though she'd be around forever, too.

The tears welled up. Julie blinked hard to stop them from flowing. She still ached almost unbearably when she thought about her sister. True, there were days, now, that passed without reminders of her. More days at a time as her death was further and further in the past. But when the hurt surfaced, it was still as fresh and raw as it had ever been.

Mary Beth would be eighteen forever. All those years she'd never live. What would she have been doing now? College? Maybe, but with a major in partying and a very minor minor in schoolwork. Julie's smile mixed with her tears. She knew her sister would have gotten along great with Dahlia. They'd probably be neck-and-neck for most famous girl on campus.

"Julie?" It was Susan Kim, pausing with her dinner tray in her hands and looking at Julie with a worried expression on her round face. "Are you all right?"

Julie brushed away her tears with the back of her hand. "Oh, hi, Susan. Yeah, I'm okay."

"Are you sure?" Susan asked softly.

Julie gave a wan nod. "Yeah. Really. Just need to take two aspirin, and I'll feel better in the morning," she joked weakly.

"Well, okay," Susan said, clearly unconvinced. She looked back at Julie as she passed through the door to the dining area. Julie forced a little smile, still feeling the tight grip of her sister's death.

She could have used a hug. Matt's hug could make the hurt go away. At least it used to be able to. Before the fighting started.

Absently, Julie filled several dozen more vegetable dishes and stocked the serving shelves, remembering how Matt had comforted her in the months right after her sister's accident. He understood how she felt, having lost his best friend, Mark, in the car with Mary Beth.

At the first None for the Road Night, the no-alcohol nights at the Fast Lane that Matt and Julie had planned in Mark and Mary Beth's memory, the DJ had put on one of Mary Beth's favorite songs. Julie had broken down, sobbing, on the dance floor. Matt had taken her outside and just held her, silently, letting her cry until there weren't any more tears left. He'd brushed the wetness from her cheeks with the tips of his fingers, lightly, tenderly caressing her face.

She wished she could feel that tender touch now. She'd turn her face up toward his and look into his eyes. Everything bad that had happened recently would dissolve into nothing. She imagined the feel of his lips as their mouths met, the warmth of his body pressed so close to hers that she could feel his heart beating. Her fingers traced the contours of his lips, his cheeks—

Julie froze, serving spoon in her hand suspended in midair. For a moment, Matt's face had disappeared, replaced in her mind's eye by Nick's. She shook her head, hard, trying to shake out the image she had no business thinking. She saw a boy in the service line looking at her, and she felt herself growing red, as if he could read her thoughts.

Nick. Lean and handsome, fine-featured with sandy-brown hair and a great smile. Subconsciously, Julie had perhaps always felt something for him that went further than simple friendship. She'd thought he was cute from the moment she first saw him, in his jeans and cowboy boots. She'd picked him out of a whole room of students waiting to register for classes at the beginning of the year. She always looked around for him in the library when she was there studying. She could spot his tall, thin frame halfway across campus.

And now, here she was daydreaming about him in the middle of the cafeteria. Daydreaming about Nick, who was Matt's friend, too. Nick, who she hoped would get together with Dahlia. She tried to imagine him kissing Dahlia instead. *Yeah, right. Admit it. You're pushing those two together because you can't go out with Nick yourself.* It wasn't an entirely new realization, Julie thought uncomfortably. But it was the first time she'd let it surface quite so plainly. She'd always told herself Nick was just a good friend. Always buried the seed of something more romantic. Was she fooling herself?

She put down the serving spoon and touched the three intertwined silver wedding bands on her left ring finger. *Past, present, and future. With Matt and Matt only. For better, for worse. For all the days of our lives.* Dutifully, Julie called up the image of Matt holding her outside the Fast Lane again. Matt, not Nick. Matt's dark hair and dark eyebrows. His deep-set eyes. His straight, broad nose and full lips, the tiny freckle at the side of his mouth.

Julie sighed. Past, present, and future—but it didn't mean that every other cute guy disappeared off the edge of the planet. You couldn't help still feeling attracted to someone else once in a while, could you? It was normal. As long as you didn't let the attraction get the better of you. As long as you remembered you were married.

* * *

Dahlia pushed open the door to the snack bar, and the first person she saw was Paul Chase. He was sitting by himself, reading. She'd barely spoken to him at all since before Thanksgiving, when he'd laid into her like a disapproving older brother. Dahlia's first thought was to turn around and go back outside.

But Madison was a small place. If she walked away now, what would she do tomorrow, or next week when she saw him again? It was time to deal. *No time like the present,* she told herself.

She walked up behind Paul and cupped her hands over his eyes. "Hey, handsome. Where've you been hiding?" she said in her friendliest, sexiest voice.

"Michelle Pfeiffer, I hope," Paul said, pulling her hands away and tipping his head back.

"How 'bout the next-best thing?" She tugged at a lock of his dark, curly hair. "Hi, Paul."

"Oh. Dahlia. I was right in the middle of some philosophy. Uh—hi."

"Long time," she said, trying to remain upbeat. "How've you been?"

"Me? Uh—okay. Fine." He turned his head back toward his book.

Total cold shoulder. Had she been that bad?

184

A month ago he'd have done anything just to hang out with her. She took a deep breath and tried again. "So, can I sit down for a minute, Paul?" she asked. "I mean, unless I'm bothering you—"

"No, I guess it's okay. Like I said, I'm just doing my philosophy reading. Meaning of existence, stuff like that. Nothing important, right?"

Dahlia sat down in the seat across from him. Uncomfortable, they exchanged a little New York gossip. Paul had seen some old neighborhood friends of Dahlia's over the break, and she brought him up to date on the gang from high school. "And Liz is still a serious trip. I mean seeee-rious," she said, hoping he would laugh along with her. But as hard as she was trying, Paul remained distant.

"Same old Liz, huh?" he said, keeping his head buried in his philosophy text. He refused to show any sign of friendliness.

Dahlia decided to give it one more try. She took his book from him and closed it. "Hey, Paul, I've got a proposition to make to you." She held out her hand. "Let's shake and be friends again."

Paul ran a hand nervously through his curly hair. His wiry frame was tight, awkward. He exhaled heavily. "About your whole act the past few months—I meant what I said, Dahlia."

"I know you did. And I've been thinking about it a lot. And, well, I'll admit that maybe I went a little overboard here at first. I guess it's just the way I am—was, I mean. I got a little wound up, you know? I suppose I was just doing what I did best because it seemed to work back in the city. You know what I mean?" She studied Paul but couldn't gauge his reaction. "I guess what I'm trying to say is, I just didn't realize how much I was flaunting the New York party girl thing. And ignoring you. I suppose I took our friendship for granted. And I'm sorry, okay? I'm really sorry, Paul." There. She'd said it. Now it was his turn to give a little.

Dahlia could see it trying to break through: the funny, old, Paul Chase smile—crinkly forehead, blinking eyelids. "Wow! Big apology, Sussman. I wish I'd had a tape recorder for that one."

"Paul, I'm serious," Dahlia said.

"Okay, okay," Paul said. "I knew you were pumping up the city chick thing big time. But you would have blown them away here without doing a thing, you know? Don't you get it? You're beautiful, and you're great just being yourself. When I yelled at you last month, I was just trying to be a real friend. And, I admit, I was a little hurt, too, when you kept ignoring me. Maybe a lot hurt. But I—"

Dahlia re-extended her hand. "Friends?"

"I really ought to make you suffer a little bit," Paul said. "But sooner or later, you know I'm going to come around," he said, shaking on the new pact. "Friends forever. Till the day we die." Finally, there it was. A big, silly, lopsided grin. The old Paul was back.

"How about after?" she asked.

"Deal." He laughed. "Although, according to what I'm reading these days, there's been this major question about that. I mean, this guy thinks I could turn into a butterfly in my next life. Or even worse, a rock or a slice of toast."

"I'll still love ya, Paul."

"Really? Even if I'm a piece of moldy white bread?"

"Hey, Dahlia!" came a shout from across the snack bar. "What about tomorrow?"

Dahlia looked over to see Jeff What's-his-name from her acting class. She shook her head. "Busy," she mouthed. She looked at Paul, rolling her eyes. "Major creep. He won't lay off about a date. Promises me the best time of my life. What a jerk, huh? I wish *he'd* turn into a rock. Like today, if possible."

Dahlia and Paul were still joking about philosophy when three guys from her history class came through the door. "Hi, Charlie!" She waved to one of them. They came over to the table.

"Hey, Dahlia, I made you a copy of our reading assignment." Charlie fumbled through his knapsack and pulled out some papers.

"You want to study for next week's test with us?" one of the other guys asked. "I've got a great apartment off campus."

"Maybe," she said, giving Paul a wink. It was nice having Paul back on her side. Just then, Nick walked through the door, looking as cute as ever. Dahlia immediately turned her attention toward him. She saw him look around the snack bar to check out the scene. He caught sight of Dahlia, and his sentiments were conveyed instantly. A frown creased his forehead and she could see the disapproval in his eyes.

Once again he'd gotten the wrong impression of her. She didn't have to try too hard to imagine what he was thinking. There she sat, surrounded by four guys, one of them smiling at her, one of them handing her something, the other two just sort of staring at her. And she was laughing and flirting back. She started to wave to Nick, but his gaze had already moved on. He waved to a table of people on the other side of the snack bar and went to sit with them.

She felt like screaming out at the top of her lungs, "I'm not what you think I am! Just give me a chance to show you!"

But what good would it do? He'd already made up his mind about her. Dahlia felt her heart sink. Then a sizzle of anger—why did she care what Nick thought? He wasn't the only cute guy in the world. There were four nice guys right here, fawning over her. So what if he was a little cuter, a little more of a mystery to her than all the other guys around? It was obvious that Nick wasn't the slightest bit interested in her. So why couldn't she just forget about him?

She just couldn't escape her own feelings. Something deep inside Dahlia told her not to let him go. There *was* something different about him, something extra special, and she could feel it. She couldn't get Nick Stone out of her mind.

Sixteen

❧

Julie sat on the sofa, hunched over the illustration in her human biology text. DNA—deoxyribonucleic acid, the double helix of life. It looked like a long, twisted ladder. *Incredible,* she thought. Studying the picture, it was hard to believe that your body was full of these ladders and that they were the basis for who you were —whether your eyes were blue or brown, whether your hair was curly or straight, maybe even why you liked broccoli but hated beets. This funny ladder was behind the whole miraculous, complicated process of life.

The sound of footsteps in the stairway leading up to the apartment brought Julie down to a more immediate reality. She looked toward the door, anticipating the sound of the bell. Matt was at work and wouldn't be home till much later. Who could it be? The doorbell sounded, one short buzz, as if the button was hot to the touch, and then a longer one.

"Who's there?" Julie called out, getting up and approaching the door. Until the attack, she hadn't even bothered to ask. Not in Madison. Not in this sweet, safe little town. The incident on the Green had changed all that.

"Julie?" came the tentative reply. "It's me— Sarah."

Julie pulled open the door. Sarah stood on the landing looking nervous, her blond hair partially covering her round face. "Hi," Julie said. Julie was surprised to see her after the uncomfortable visit to Sarah's dorm room. Something was definitely up.

"Julie, I need to talk to you," Sarah said, her voice urgent. "Am I interrupting anything?"

Julie shook her head and opened the door wide to let Sarah through. "Just trying to get some studying done so I can go to that party at Manning tonight. Come on in."

Sarah came into the living room and glanced around. "Matt's not home?"

"Work," Julie answered. "What's up?" Sarah looked extremely tense. More bad news? Julie steeled herself.

"It's about the guy they're looking for," Sarah said.

Julie could feel every muscle in her body begin to tighten. "Carl Sever? Did he turn up?"

Sarah pressed her lips together. The room seemed to swell with silence. Finally, she spoke. "He's not the one," she said, shaking her head. "They're looking for the wrong guy."

"They are?" Julie was hit with a wave of surprise. So Matt was right! "Are you telling me you know who it was?" Her surprise deepened.

Sarah nodded, shamefaced. "I was so afraid to say anything." Tears were forming in the corners of her eyes, and she struggled with her words. "It's just like what you said in your article. I was afraid to tell what really happened." Sarah wrapped her arms around herself as if for protection. "I don't know. Maybe it was my own fault. Before anything happened, I had been talking to the guy, the one who did it, I mean. We were laughing together, having fun. He seemed really nice at first." The tears were rolling down her cheeks now, and she spoke haltingly. "If my brother knew . . ." Her words dissolved in a torrent of sobs.

Julie put a gentle hand on Sarah's shoulder. If her brother knew? Was the person who had attacked Sarah a friend of Tim's? A college guy?

Sarah's sobs subsided under Julie's touch. "I just couldn't tell anyone. I was too afraid. I didn't know if people would believe me. I mean, everyone likes the guy. They all think he's great. Even Tim. And they all saw me with him at Tim's party." Sarah's voice started spiraling out of control again, her words piling on top of each other in a rush of emotion.

Julie tried to calm her down. "Hey, it's going to be okay," she said, hoping her own words were true. She led Sarah over to the sofa and sat her down, sitting by her side to keep a comforting arm around her. "What *did* happen? You can tell me, Sarah."

Sarah shook her head over and over. "I wanted to keep it a secret, but I just can't keep it inside anymore. It's just not right." Her lower lip trembled. "Not if it means they're going to find that guy from town and arrest him."

"Sarah, you can trust me. Who was it?" Julie asked, curiosity mixing with dread.

"Okay." She sighed, exhaling deeply, like a balloon deflating. "We were at my brother's house off campus. Everyone was getting back from Thanksgiving vacation, and he wanted to have a welcome-home kind of thing. Mostly it was the guys from the football team and some of their girlfriends. Anyway, there was this one guy—Tommy Brady—Brady they call him." Sarah's voice dropped to a whisper.

"That's his name? He's the one who did it?" Julie asked.

Sarah nodded. "He's one of my brother's teammates. Big deal around campus. Anyway, we were getting along pretty well—at least I thought we were—and he was paying all this special attention to me. I guess, well, I felt kind of flattered." Julie could hear the bitterness in Sarah's words. "What an idiot I was," Sarah went on. "But I'm a freshman, and he's a junior, and he could have been talking to someone else."

Sarah took a deep breath and continued. "Maybe I was leading him on or something. I don't know. I thought I was just having a good time. He asked me back to his room." She swallowed hard. "I said no. I'd only talked to him that one night, and, well, maybe some people think it's old-fashioned of me . . ."

Julie shook her head. "No way. It's not old-fashioned at all."

"Anyhow, I left by myself, and I started walking back to the dorm, and the next thing I knew . . ." Sarah's words trailed off. "You know the rest of it."

"Oh, you poor thing," Julie said.

"Then you don't think that because I was flirting with him it was my fault?"

Julie shook her head. "Absolutely not. You said no. No means no!"

Sarah shrugged. "Yeah. It's just that when it was happening to me, I felt so—I don't know, guilty. Like if this awful thing was happening, I must have done something to deserve it. And then, the guy was Tim's friend and everything."

"Only because no one knew what he was really like." Julie shuddered.

Sarah nodded slowly. "Then right before he ran away, he told me I'd better not say a word to anyone."

Julie sucked in her breath.

Sarah nodded. "He said no one would believe me anyway."

"I believe you, Sarah," Julie said grimly. "You can't let him get away with that. What if he does something like that again?" Julie felt frightened —for Sarah and for anyone else who might cross paths with this Brady guy.

"I know. That's why I've decided to go to the police," Sarah said. "To speak out, like you said I should do in your article. So they don't arrest the wrong guy. And so Brady doesn't hurt anybody else." She paused, and the corners of her mouth turned down. "The only thing is, I'd feel a lot less scared if I didn't have to go alone. . . ."

"I'll get my coat," Julie said immediately. She thought about why the wrong guy had been a suspect in the first place, and she felt a cramp of awful responsibility. "Going down to the police station with you is the least I can do," she said.

At first glance, it seemed like a regular evening at the Barn and Grill. Blue-jeaned, T-shirted, and work boot–clad townies sat on one side drinking beer and eating burgers. The college students on the other side of the restaurant differed in their dress code and their beverage selection—the under-twenty-one crowd going for soft drinks instead of beer. Usually, the two groups studiously ignored each other. But that night, there was a growing undercurrent of tension.

"I know those are his friends. They'll know where he's hiding," Matt overheard one of the college kids, a huge guy wearing a crimson and white rugby shirt, say to his friends. He stared across the room and raised his voice. "Come on, let's just make them tell us."

"Sounds like college boy has a little problem," said a burly man in a leather vest, his voice equally loud.

Matt felt as if he were wading through a mine field. One extra step in the wrong direction and the Barn and Grill would explode. Leon and Nick might have thought that the town-gown thing wasn't anything to worry about, but Matt could feel that it had reached a peak, and he was stuck in the middle of it all.

"Burgers are ready, Matt," Pat called to him through the opening between the kitchen and the restaurant. There was an extra degree of tension in her voice. Jake, too, normally so open and easygoing, worked the bar with a guarded expression. It had been like that for the past few days.

Matt felt terrible—and responsible. Ever since Julie's article, the Barn and Grill had reeked of anger and fear. And it was all because Matt had told Julie about Carl. Matt collected the hamburgers and brought them over to Marcy and the faded-jeans girls. "Here's your burger, Marcy. Medium well with fries."

He'd gotten used to her table's recent cold-shoulder treatment, so he ignored Marcy's friend when she muttered the word *traitor* under her breath.

"Your beer's coming," he said flatly.

197

"Thanks a lot, rat—I mean Matt," Marcy said. Her friends laughed sarcastically.

"Hey, come on, Marcy," Matt said. "How much longer are you going to—?" But before Matt could finish his sentence, the door swung open and Carl stood there, fire and rage pulsating through every vein. A hush descended on the Barn and Grill, as heads turned in Carl's direction. Only the wail of the country song on the jukebox broke through the silence in the room.

"That's him!" the guy in the rugby shirt shouted. He and his two friends jumped to their feet.

Carl stood there, a defiant look on his face. He reached into his jacket pocket and took out a shiny flask. He unscrewed the top and took a big swig, then exhaled loudly. "Shut up," he snapped.

He walked over to the three guys on the college side. "Well, well, well. If it ain't the lynching squad. Kiddies from campus send you out to find me? Well, here I am." He grinned and held up his hands, miming surrender. "There's just one thing you might want to know. I didn't do a blasted thing!"

"That's not the way we heard it," said a short guy in a green sweater.

"Well, then, I guess you heard wrong," Carl shot back at them.

"Then why did you leave town so fast?"

"Maybe I went to visit my sick grandmother," Carl said with a laugh. "I don't suppose any of you know a guy named Brady? Tommy Brady? College guy."

The Madison students looked at one another, their faces showing both confusion and anger. "Brady?"

"Yeah, that's right." Carl sauntered over to the college side. "I figured you'd know who I was talking about. Tommy Brady. Sweet kid, huh? He's down at the station right now confessing to the cops. Your buddy Brady's the one who attacked that girl."

Matt was startled. *A college guy. What do you know!*

"Brady? That's bull," said the guy in the green sweater, getting up from his chair and shoving Carl backward a few steps. "You're a liar, Sever," he shouted.

"And you're a fool," Carl shouted back. He looked over toward a group of guys on the town side and gave them the signal. They were up out of their seats in a flash, backing up Carl. Carl took another swig of whiskey, then put his flask back in his jacket pocket. "Whenever you're ready," he said with a sneer, pumping his fist in his palm.

Within seconds, six enraged guys were going at one another full force. The rest of the patrons backed up against the walls. In the confusion there were the sounds of broken glass shattering on the floor and a few panicked cries.

Carl threw a series of furious, drunken punches at the rugby-shirted guy, who was nearly twice his size. A few missed, but one managed to land solidly on his jaw. The guy hit back hard with a blow to Carl's mouth, drawing a trace of blood. Carl dropped to the ground, burying his head in his hands. Someone cracked a chair—against someone else? It was impossible for Matt to tell in all the chaos that had broken loose.

In a matter of minutes, all of them, town and college, were on the ground, a massive heap of writhing arms and legs accompanied by grunts and groans.

Matt jumped in. He had to stop the fight. "Break it up!" he shouted as he worked his way into the pile. He tried to pry the bodies apart, dodging flailing fists, elbows, and knees. He felt a jab in the ribs. Someone kicked him solidly in the lower back. Matt spun around, ready to throw a punch of his own, but he saw he was face-to-face with Pat. She and Jake had joined Matt in the effort to stop the fighting.

"Get off me," came a scream from the bottom of the pile. Matt yanked at a Madison jersey and got elbowed in the chest. He winced in pain but held on tight.

Somehow, Jake had managed to subdue Carl's big, leather-clad buddy. Jake had him pinned facedown on the floor, his knee pressed firmly into his back. Finally, with the help of a few others in the restaurant, they managed to separate the two raging factions. Matt, Pat, and Jake stood between them.

"I still say it was you. You did it," one of the college guys jeered. "You did it, Sever, and you're going to pay."

"That's enough!" Jake shouted. "Enough. You want to continue this fight? There's the street," he said, pointing to the door. "Now get out of my place. All of you."

There was a low murmur of voices. "You okay, Frank?" Marcy asked one of Carl's friends.

"I can't believe it was one of us!" a shocked college boy said, shaking his head. "Brady? He's in my English class."

Matt looked around. A couple of smashed

beer mugs, a bloodstain on the wood floor, a broken chair. At least they hadn't brought the walls down.

"We knew it was one of your own," one of Marcy's friends sneered. "Figures."

"Please," Pat begged. "I think it'd be best if we all went home."

"I think that's a good idea," Jake said. "The Barn and Grill is closed, as of right now."

Matt could tell that Pat was near tears. He raced over to the front door and opened it. "You heard her. Time to say good night, everybody." The crowd exited quietly without another incident.

As the last of them left, Pat came over and slammed the door shut. Matt walked over to the broken chair and knelt down next to it, making a futile attempt to piece it back together. "I'm really sorry," Matt said.

"Sorry? About what?" Jake asked. "It seems to me you were the first one to try and stop those guys."

"Yeah, but the whole thing probably wouldn't have happened if it weren't for me. I mean, Julie and I got Carl dragged into this whole thing. Carl and the Barn and Grill."

Jake shook his head. "Matt, this isn't your

fault. It was bound to happen sooner or later. That's just the way things are around here."

"Actually, I think we were lucky. Could have been a lot worse, huh, Jake?" Pat said.

He nodded. "Don't worry, Matt, they'll all be back, you'll see. Where else do they have to go, anyway? I wouldn't be surprised if Carl's in here by tomorrow afternoon, just as soon as he gets off work. As if nothing happened. And the college kids'll be back, too. I'd bet on it. Let's just clean up the mess, okay?"

"Maybe I should apologize to Carl," Matt said.

"After what he said about Julie?" Pat asked. "He's not worth your breath. Come on, Matt, give yourself a break. You didn't do anything wrong."

"I guess." Matt sighed. Tommy Brady. Maybe it should have made Matt feel better to know it was a college student, but it didn't. Sarah had still been a victim, and Matt still felt sickened by the split between the students and residents of Madison.

He got up and went into the kitchen to get the mop and bucket. Perhaps Jake and Pat were right. Perhaps the fighting was unavoidable. Matt had witnessed plenty of barroom brawls at the Fast Lane that had been far more violent. At least tonight nobody had pulled a knife, or even worse, a gun.

Still, he felt that this fight was more than just ugly. It wasn't the typical drunken blowup over some old grudge or a heated argument between two friends. This one was different. Town versus gown. Gown against town. Little Madison, Ohio, torn right down the middle by narrowness and misunderstanding. And Julie determinedly on one side and Matt stuck someplace in no-man's-land. He felt trapped, with no way out.

Seventeen

They were both right. Julie hurried along the side of the road that led out of town. The Barn and Grill was a long walk, and the night was bitter with a freezing wind, but Julie couldn't wait to talk to Matt. She turned up the collar of her pea jacket, stepping off the shoulder of the road as a car whizzed past her.

Matt was right about the fact that she had jumped to conclusions. Practically everybody had. At the same time, Julie was right to coax Sarah out of her silence, and about the need for her to speak out.

They were both right, and now that the truth was out, she hoped they could begin to put the ugliness behind them. To make up and recapture the love and joy they'd shared when they said "I do" in the sunny, wood-walled room by the brook. Julie knew why you pledged your love for better or for worse. These past few weeks had definitely counted on the worse side. But two years of love and tenderness and friendship were too special to throw away, Julie reminded herself. It was why she and Matt had married in the first place.

Her breath made little puffs of steam under the streetlights. Was it really only a few weeks since she and Matt had celebrated their one-month anniversary, since they'd held each other in the starlight as if there were no one else in the world?

Julie thought about the way he had kissed her that night, his lips tasting of sweet cider. Her step quickened. Maybe after Matt got off work, they'd go to the party at Manning together and dance and look into each other's eyes, and Matt would be the most special person in her world again. Maybe then she'd stop daydreaming about Nick and forget about townies and gownies and the harsh words that she and Matt had exchanged since the night they'd found Sarah on the Green. Forget the hurt of sleeping with a wall between her and Matt.

She turned right at the gas station, which was locked up for the night, and headed up a side street toward the Barn and Grill. She came over a slight rise, and the former barn loomed into sight. It seemed eerily quiet for a Friday night. No strains of music floated out over the darkened fields, no sound of laughter or voices. And the lights in the main room of the restaurant were dim. Only the kitchen lights stood out bright against the night.

Julie jogged the few yards to the Barn and Grill's driveway. But as she headed for the door, she heard the throaty metal purr of a motorcycle being revved up. Matt's motorcycle. She whirled around and spotted his familiar, athletic silhouette astride his Harley in the parking lot at the side of the restaurant.

"Matt!" she called out, racing toward him. "Matt!" She waved.

"Julie." Something in his voice stopped her in her tracks just before she threw her arms around him in a hug.

"What's going on?" she asked, a flutter of nervousness starting in her stomach.

"Going on? Nothing. Not anymore. It's over, and I'm out of here," Matt responded tightly.

"Out of here? Where are you going? Don't you have to work?" The nervousness raced through Julie's whole body.

"We had to close down early," Matt said curtly. "Big fight."

"About what?" Julie asked. Why was Matt acting this way?

"About Carl Sever being innocent. In case you're interested, it was one of *your* college boys that night on the Green."

Julie swallowed. "I know. That's what I came to tell you. The whole thing's finally over. Aren't you happy about that?"

"Yeah. Ecstatic," Matt said bitingly. "It's so over that a bunch of Madison jocks and a bunch of Carl's buddies were going at each other in there like they wanted to kill each other. If you hadn't written that article—"

"Sarah might never have told the real story," Julie cut him off. His anger stung her. And she felt herself growing angry, too.

Matt gave a faint, grim shrug. His motorcycle hummed beneath him. "All I know is I go into work, and it's like a war zone. I'm caught in the middle, and it stinks."

"Look, I'm sorry about the fight. Really I am," she said tensely. "But does it have to destroy us? I came over here to try to put an end to all the fighting. All *our* fighting."

"So I'm supposed to forget about everything that's gone on? Just like that, pretend it never happened?"

Julie took a step toward Matt. "I just don't

want to let anything get in between us anymore, that's all." She made one more effort to reach out to him. "Listen, whatever went on in there," she gestured at the Barn and Grill, "you've got the rest of the night off. Why don't we get dressed up and go over to that party on North Campus? They're having a live band. Come on, Matt, a party. We used to be pretty good at those." She held her breath.

"Great." Matt practically spat out the word. "A college party. Just what I need to help me feel even more out of place around here. Forget it, Julie."

"Well, maybe if you'd try a little . . ." Julie felt a swell of frustration and anger. Why had she bothered? Why had she walked all the way out here? Matt seemed to want to stay angry forever.

The stars overhead burned cold and sharp. "Look, Julie, I just need to be alone," he said. He gunned his engine. "I'll drop you off at home—or at that party. Wherever."

"And where are you going?"

"For a ride."

Julie turned on her heel. "Forget it, Matt. I'll walk," she said. She'd tried. She'd tried and Matt hadn't given an inch. If he was going to act like he didn't need her, she could darned well do the same.

Matt shrugged. "Suit yourself." He raced his engine and shot out across the Barn and Grill parking lot with a peal of tires.

Julie watched him roar off. As angry as she felt, she couldn't hold back a tidal wave of hurt. If Matt would just turn around and ride back to her, she'd forget all the fighting. If he'd just come back. But he rode on, until the sound of his bike faded in the winter night.

Marion inhaled a deep breath of fresh night air. An exhilarating coldness, a round, yellow-orange moon overhead, the warmth of Fred's hand in hers—finally they'd found the perfect moment for a date. And the perfect place, too. The manicured, outdoor sculpture garden of the Madison College Art Museum made Marion feel as if she'd been whisked away from Ohio and dropped down in the most romantic spot in France or Italy.

She felt a nervous thrill. She and Fred were the only ones in the garden. And tonight, there were no bio reviews, no half-dissected crayfish or earthworms, no one describing the mating habits of invertebrate mammals at the front of a lecture hall.

"Oooh, let's see what's down there," she said, pointing to a narrow walkway lined by spotlighted bronze and marble statues and tall, sculptured evergreen hedges.

"Wow, it looks like some sort of maze," Fred said. "Think we'll find our way out?"

The pathway wound to an end, spiraling in on a secluded spot that showcased a life-size, abstract bronze statue of a woman reclining. Hidden away from the rest of the world by the hedges, the sculpture was chiseled in geometric shapes suggesting head, torso, arms, legs, and breasts. The moonlight cast the sculpture in a golden, shimmery glow. Marion could just make out the title that was etched into the stone base: "The Ideal Form."

"Wow, I can't believe somebody really made something this beautiful," Marion said.

"And look at the way it's oxidizing. I'll bet it's been outside for at least fifteen years. I heard that the bronze gets more valuable with age," Fred said. He put his hand on the dark metal foot. "It's so smooth."

Marion took a few steps back and sat down on a little stone bench positioned opposite the sculpture.

"Marion?" Fred said softly, sitting down by her side.

211

"Yeah?"

"So—so are you. Beautiful, I mean."

Marion felt her face grow hot. She could barely believe her ears. "Do you really think so?" Fred nodded. "That's so sweet."

Marion felt his closeness. But she could sense his nervousness beginning to build, too.

"Um—I do. Um—yes, I do mean it, about you," he said, getting more jittery with each word.

Uh-oh. He started tapping one of his feet on the ground, and then she noticed his hand reaching for a tug at his baseball cap. Except he wasn't even wearing a cap tonight. Bad news. Fred was two seconds away from the twenty-minute stare at his loafers. *No way. Not this time. Go get him!* she told herself, remembering Gwen's coaching. She reached out and took his hand again.

He looked at her. She smiled, slid over as near to him as she could, and turned her face up toward his. She had gotten this close; now it was up to him to go the final few inches. She closed her eyes. She waited. There was a brief, awkward pause. She was afraid that he'd chicken out again. But then she felt his lips press against hers. One, two, three short kisses. The next one lasted longer. His lips were as soft as she'd imagined they would be.

Marion reached up and wound her arms around him, drawing him even closer. She felt his hands gently caressing her face. They kissed again. And again, and again. Marion let her fingers run through Fred's hair. It was so soft and fine. His lips tasted a little minty, like mouthwash or toothpaste—maybe he'd been hoping for a full-fledged kiss tonight, too! He smelled good, and his kisses were perfect. Not that Marion had anything to compare them to, but she didn't need any comparison. Everything felt amazing. Nothing could be better than Fred's deepening embrace.

She tilted her head back, staring up at the night sky as Fred planted gentle kisses on her face and neck. Even the moon winked back at her. And then their mouths met again. Time slipped away.

They might have kept kissing all night if it had been just a little warmer, but as a chilly wind blew, Marion felt an involuntary shiver run up her back.

"You're cold," Fred said, full of concern. "Here, wear my jacket over yours." He quickly unzipped his plaid, wool jacket and wrapped it around her. "Better?" he asked.

Marion nodded. But she was sure Fred would be shivering in a minute. He had on only a flannel shirt. She pulled him close and gave him a soft kiss on the forehead. "Now you're going to freeze, Fred. Maybe we should go inside. Hey, I know. How about we go over to De-Caff for a cup of hot chocolate?"

"I could stay here all night with you." Fred smiled. "But I guess it's pretty cold. I mean, you can still wear the jacket, of course, but the hot chocolate is a good idea. Can I treat you?"

Hand in hand, they followed the path that wound away from paradise. Marion looked back once at "The Ideal Form." She wondered if one day she'd talk about this place the way her mother talked about the swing in the gazebo where she'd first kissed her father.

Dreamily, Marion and Fred made their way back to the main garden area. But Marion felt herself plummet down to earth as she noticed that all the lights inside the museum had been shut off. And—oh no!—a wrought-iron security gate had been pulled closed, covering the glass door that led back inside the museum! The solid black bars were a sure sign of trouble.

Fred noticed, too. "Oops," he said, glancing at his thick, multifunction watch. "Eleven eighteen. They've been closed for nearly forty minutes." He dropped Marion's hand and ran over to the door. "Hello!" he called out, shaking the iron bars. No answer. "Wow, I think we're really locked out. I mean we're locked in. Hello?" he tried again.

Marion raced over and put her hand through the space between the bars and started banging on the glass, but there was no response. "Oh, no," she moaned. She looked all around her, but there was no way out. "What are we going to do, Fred? It's like wall-to-wall hedges. And there's a giant fence around the whole place." The hedges that lined the garden on three sides were way over her head, and behind them, she could see the sharp spikes of the iron bars. "I can climb trees, but not these things. Besides, I'd probably get skewered by those spears on top of the fence."

"Yeah, and you'd need suction cups for feet to climb the museum walls," Fred said. "You'd have to be some kind of human insect."

Hopeless. "Hello?!" they called once more, screaming at the tops of their lungs together. But it was no use. They knew they were stuck.

"Hey, don't worry," Fred said. Marion could tell he was trying to sound brave. "I'll bet there's a security check in a few hours. Somebody will be by. Don't you think?" he added hopefully.

"You mean you think they send someone around to make sure nobody tries to steal a two-ton bronze statue?" Marion asked.

"Well, they must have this place locked up for a reason," Fred said. Marion noticed his teeth were beginning to chatter.

"Oh, hey, here." She began to give his jacket back.

"Wait, we can share it," Fred said, putting his arms around her, inside the jacket.

Marion felt a thrill of warmth. At least she and Fred were stuck here together. She turned her face up to kiss him. It looked as though she was going to have some story to tell.

Eighteen

❧

Julie pulled open the door to Manning Hall and was hit with an instant burst of noise and warmth. The music seemed to swell as she stepped inside the crowded entranceway and pulled off her gloves. *Boy, is it ever packed in here,* she thought.

She rubbed her hands together, trying to take off the chill from her long walk from the Barn and Grill. She looked around. There were so many people spilling out of the main room that she could barely get more than a few feet inside, let alone get a view of the dance floor or try to find anyone she knew. In front of her, two couples stood with paper drinking cups. "I heard he tried to convince the police that *she* made the first move," one of the boys was saying.

"I still can't believe the guy was from the college," one of the girls added.

Julie squeezed by them. She couldn't seem to get away from the subject. She swallowed hard. The cold had numbed just about everything but the pain of Matt's brush-off. Was it so wrong of her to think they could put the ugliness of the town-gown tension behind them? To pick up where they had left off on that clear, cold, perfect night at the quarry when they'd toasted to one month of marriage?

She wound her way through the throng of partiers toward the main room. A boy jostled past her, his drink sloshing out of his cup and onto the floor. Julie sidestepped the mess and made her way to where she had a view of the sea of bodies moving to the music. Dahlia was supposed to be here somewhere, and Nick and some of her friends from her old hall. Julie searched the crowd. She couldn't find any of them, although it seemed as if everyone else on campus was there. She looked out at the crowd of dancers for Nick. His tall head must be popping up somewhere. Was he out on that packed floor with some pretty girl? She didn't see him.

But there was a familiar face—Dahlia's old friend Paul stood behind the drink table mixing more punch. He lived in a divided double up-

218

stairs and looked to be on the refreshment committee. If anyone would know where Dahlia was, Paul would.

Julie snaked through the crowd to where he stood, pouring a bottle of ginger ale into the huge bowl. "Hi, Paul!" She tried her best to sound cheerful, even though her words with Matt hung over her like a storm cloud.

"Julie! Hey, party down!" Paul said.

"You seen Dahlia around anywhere?" she asked in a false, bright voice.

Paul reached under the table and brought up a gallon container of orange juice. "Not yet. Fashionably late, I guess. It's a New York thing. You know how she is. Bummer!" He shook the juice carton, but only a thin trickle came out. "Out of O.J. Listen, I've got to make a run to get some more. Catch you in a bit, okay?"

"Okay." Julie nodded.

"Hey, Julie, are you all right?" Paul gave her a hard look.

She conjured up a toothpaste smile. "Sure I am. Sure. You go ahead. People are going to get thirsty." Then she was alone again. Alone in a throng of laughing, yelling, dancing people. The band was playing a reggae tune, the amps turned up so high, Julie could feel the beat through the soles of her sneakers. She moved around a little to the music, trying to get in the mood, but she felt self-conscious. She unbuttoned her coat but didn't take it off, sticking her hands in the pockets so she wouldn't have to figure out what to do with them.

A few people waved or said hello as they walked by her—leftover attention from the fame of her article—but mostly people were busy with their own friends, partying and dancing.

Julie felt a little bit the way she had at the beginning of the year, when Matt was still in Philadelphia, and she would go to a party and watch the couples dance, and pretend to have fun, while her heart was really somewhere else.

Except back in the fall at least she'd been able to run home and call Matt and hear him tell her he loved her. Then she'd been able to count the days until she saw him again, until they were together and everything was perfect.

Julie felt the salty sting of tears in her eyes. Was she ever going to feel that way about him again? She'd tried tonight. She'd reached out. But Matt had turned away. She didn't even understand where they'd started to go wrong. Back in high school, any problems going on around them had only brought them closer together. Why was it so different now?

Julie's tears were flowing, and she couldn't stop them. She stood in the middle of the crowded room with the driving music, not even bothering to brush away the liquid tracks of her unhappiness.

And then she felt him, even before she turned to see him. Nick was coming toward her, edging his way to her side. "Julie! Hey, what's wrong?" He put a warm hand on her shoulder.

It only made the tears come faster. And suddenly, without quite knowing how, she was sobbing in his arms, her head against the soft cotton of his shirt. Wordlessly, he stroked her hair and held her as she cried. It was all coming out —all the tension and fear and bad feelings. It felt so good to just cry.

Nick's shirt was wet by the time she felt her sobs quieting. She turned her face up to him and saw the concern in his green eyes. "I'm sorry," she said as he gently released her. Around them, a few people cast curious looks at them, but most of the partiers were more interested in squeezing by them to get to the dance floor or the refreshment table.

"Nothing to be sorry about. What's going on?" Nick asked, his concerned voice rising over the music.

Julie shrugged.

"Come on, you can tell me, Julie. What is it?"

"Big problems."

"You and Matt?"

She nodded.

"Can you talk about it?"

Julie sniffled. "I guess. But I'll probably start crying again."

"What are friends for?" Nick said. "Let's go outside where it's quieter."

"I'd like to get out of here," Julie said, "but I'm just starting to defrost. I had to walk all the way from the Barn and Grill."

"Uh-oh. It does sound bad," Nick said.

Julie nodded. "Yeah. You know, what I could really go for is something warm to drink from De-Caff. No, on second thought, if there's comedy there tonight, I don't think it's the place for me."

Nick nodded. "Especially the brand of comedy at De-Caff. It can be pretty sour sometimes. Listen, if you want, we can go across to my dorm. I've got this really awful hot-chocolate mix, but it'll be quiet and warm."

"Sounds like just what I need." Julie felt herself break into a little smile. "I'll take it."

"The room's kind of a mess," he warned her.

"That's okay. So am I," she joked wanly.

As they crossed North Quad, she told him what had gone on with Matt, her hurt and anger rising again as she recounted how he had ridden away from her. Nick listened sympathetically as he led the way to his room.

A few minutes later, she was sitting on the edge of his unmade bed. Nick had an open double with a guy from Cleveland, and the main decor on both sides seemed to be piles of clothes, books, and CDs. But it was warm and quiet as he'd promised, and Julie was glad to be away from the crowd.

Nick sat cross-legged on the floor, holding an electric immersion coil in a mug of water. "From everything you're telling me, and from what Matt's said, too, it sounds like what happened to that girl on the Green set off a bunch of other stuff." As the water bubbled up around the edges of the mug, he unplugged the immersion coil and ripped open a packet of instant hot chocolate.

"What do you mean?" Julie asked.

He stirred the drink and handed her the steaming mug. "Look, Julie. I'm the first to admit that maybe I'm a little envious of you and Matt," Nick said. He shrugged. "But at the same time, it can't be the easiest thing in the world to be the only ones around who are married."

"It's not." Julie held the warm mug in her palms and took a sip of the hot chocolate. "Blah. This *is* pretty bad." She gave a little laugh. "Aren't you going to have any?"

Nick shook his head and laughed, too. He balled up the empty cocoa packet and shot it into the wastebasket in the corner of the room. "I don't know about you, but I kind of think it's been a big enough deal getting used to the first year of college," he said, coming over and sitting down next to her. "Trying to make a life with someone, too—I can't really imagine it."

"Maybe we couldn't, either," Julie said. "I mean, I don't really know what I expected. We didn't really think about it. We just sort of did it. One minute I'm on the back of his Harley riding to Maryland, and the next minute I'm a married woman!"

Nick was quiet for a moment. "And you're sorry?" he asked softly.

Julie felt a wave of misery. "I'm afraid to think about it." She put her mug of hot chocolate down on the floor next to her.

Nick nodded. "We all go around pretending we're on our own around here. But look, as much as I don't like to admit it, my folks are still sending me an allowance. And you *know* I've got plenty of company. Let's face it, you guys are the only ones who are really on your own."

"I wish I wasn't," Julie said. The words just slipped out. "I wish I was just like everyone else around here." And suddenly she was trying to fight off another bout of crying.

"Hey," Nick said, leaning forward and brushing the new tears from the corners of her eyes. His touch was light and tender. He let his hand rest on her face.

Nick was so sweet. Julie reached up and covered his hand with her own. She looked into his eyes and smiled through her tears. He smiled back, leaning toward her, ever so slightly. She felt herself straining closer to him. They drew nearer. She could feel it happening, and she didn't want to stop it. Their lips met. She felt her whole body tingle with a kind of forbidden pleasure. Their kiss was soft and lingering. It was all wrong, yet it felt so right.

But suddenly Nick pulled back. He took his hands off her. "I shouldn't have done that."

Julie felt a crash of emotions—disappointment, relief, but mostly an uncontrollable feeling of yearning. She wanted Nick's lips on hers again. She wanted another moment where all the rules were gone, the sweetness of their kiss overpowering everything else so that nothing else mattered. She wanted to give in to her feelings for Nick, to feel him close to her again, to feel him wanting her.

She put her palm to his cheek. He didn't resist. She let her fingers slide to his lips, tracing the contours of his slightly open mouth. She could feel herself trembling. She hesitated, but only for a second. Then she brought her lips to his again. She kissed him softly, gently brushing her mouth over his. His lips were so soft, but with the roughness of stubble above his top lip. She kissed him again. He responded, his lips hot and wet. She wound her arms around him and let loose all the feelings she'd been holding back.

They drew each other down onto the bed, one kiss melting into the next.

Nineteen

❧

The night was winding down at the Manning party. The band shifted into their soft, romantic sound, a soothing Caribbean beat filtering through the room. Dahlia was dancing with Jeff, pressed tightly against his large-framed body. But she felt far from soothed.

How did she always end up in these situations? Jeff X. She didn't even know his last name. And she didn't even care. But she'd spent the last hour dancing with anybody who'd asked her. It was all she could do to try to blow off some steam after seeing Julie and Nick leaving the party together looking as if they were a lot more than just friends.

Dahlia had come to the party dressed to the hilt, with hopes of making Nick look twice. She had decided that it was time to give it her best college try. But that was before she'd spotted them—Julie, with her head buried in Nick's chest, and Nick, with his arms wrapped tightly around Julie. They were so involved with each other that they hadn't even noticed Dahlia coming into the party. Then, a few minutes later, she'd watched them leave together, arm in arm, oblivious to the rest of the world.

She couldn't believe it. Julie, her married friend, and Nick. How could Julie do it? There had to be a mistake. But through the windows of the Manning lounge, Dahlia had watched them head in the direction of Nick's dorm.

Maybe she should have read the signs—the way Julie was always talking about how terrific Nick was, how cute he was. As for Nick, his feelings for Julie were pretty obvious if you stopped to think about it.

Dahlia thought about how Julie was always pushing her and Nick together, when what Julie really wanted was to have Nick for herself. Swaying in Jeff's arms, Dahlia felt a wave of resentment toward Julie. Okay, so she and Matt had been fighting a little, but so what? All married couples argued. Dahlia couldn't believe that Julie was the type to find pleasure elsewhere. No matter how she tossed it around in her head, Dahlia just couldn't make sense of what she'd seen. Julie already had a guy. A guy who loved her so much he'd decided to spend the rest of his life with her.

The soft wail of a trumpet echoed through the room. "A little love song, to get you all into the mood," the bandleader cooed. "Into the mood for love. Mmmm, get a little closer," he whispered into the microphone.

Dahlia felt Jeff X tugging at the back of her dress, his hands trying to get where they weren't invited. "Come closer, baby," he muttered. She reached behind her and tried to bat his roaming hands away.

"Jeff, no," she told him flatly. As if he were deaf, he maintained his clutching, suffocating hold on her. Why did she have to wind up with such a loser for the slow dances? She looked around at the other couples. A pair she recognized from her English class was lost in a passionate embrace. Dahlia steamed, imagining that Nick and Julie might be lost in one of their own at this very minute.

"Yeah, you've got it. You've got it all, Dahlia," Jeff groaned in her ear, giving her a kiss.

Dahlia felt a tear trickle down her cheek. The truth was, Julie was the one who had it all. And then some. A loving husband, an A average, all that attention from her newspaper article, and now she even had Nick, the guy Dahlia wanted for herself. For a brief moment, Dahlia found herself wishing she hadn't paid Julie's tuition. That secret deed. And why? So Julie could stick around Madison and steal the guy Dahlia had her eye on?

Except that Julie really hadn't stolen anyone. Nick wasn't interested in Dahlia to begin with. And Julie had no idea that Dahlia liked him, too. If anything, it was Nick who was doing the stealing.

Dahlia felt another wet, Jeff X kiss on the side of her neck and her cheek. She picked her head up and saw Jeff's yearning eyes. Did he really think she was as beautiful and incredible as he kept whispering in her ear? Dahlia wished she liked him more. As he pulled her a little closer, she felt herself start to give in. She closed her eyes. But the instant she felt his lips, a tear slid down her face.

"Excuse me," Dahlia heard a familiar voice say. "Mind if I cut in?" She picked her head up to see Paul Chase.

"Yeah, actually I do," Jeff snarled. He waved Paul away. "Butt out, pal." He tried to keep his hold on Dahlia, but she pulled away from him.

"No, it's okay," Dahlia said, wiping her eyes.

"I've really had a lot of fun, Jeff, but Paul's an old friend. I promised him a dance."

She grabbed hold of Paul as if he were a life raft. Jeff X shook his head in confusion, shrugged, and walked away, immediately searching the room for a replacement. "Not a moment too soon, Chase," she whispered in his ear. "Thanks a lot." She wrapped her arms tightly around Paul.

"Hey, you know slow dancing's not really my thing, but I saw you looking so totally bummed with that lug-brain. I hope you can deal with my stepping on your toes a little."

"Step all you want, Paul. I could use an old friend more than ever right now."

"Hey, what's the matter, Dahlia? I've known you long enough to know that it's more than just that geek-face. You sure you're okay?"

"No, I'm not sure about anything. Just hold on, Chase, okay?" she said, sniffling the last of her tears. She kept her arms wrapped around Paul and rested her head on his shoulder.

It had taken all night, but at least Dahlia had wound up in the arms of a true friend. Somebody who knew her and understood her. She was thankful that Paul was there for her. He was the only person on campus she felt she could really count on. Maybe it took going to kindergarten with someone to really be able to trust him.

The soothing sounds of the Caribbean beat were finally working. It felt a little strange being in Paul's arms, but it was a comforting kind of strange. She held on tightly, and it felt good. She closed her eyes and, finally, let herself relax. Her body pressed against Paul's. Without really thinking about it, her fingers wandered up and down his back. She stroked his soft, thick curls.

"Dahlia?" Paul sounded a little startled.

Dahlia picked her head up off his shoulder and looked into Paul's eyes. Familiar brown doe eyes, framed by a crinkly brow and an adorable, crooked smile. *Why not?* she thought. She reached up on her tiptoes and gave Paul a light kiss on the mouth.

Paul quivered, his eyes widening with surprise. "Ding, ding, ding—jackpot! Heaven can wait, everything's just fine down here."

Dahlia laughed. "Can't you just be quiet and kiss me again?"

Paul's fingers traced a line across her cheeks, her chin, and came to rest on her lips. Dahlia kissed them softly. Paul smiled. Their mouths came together again. Their second kiss was longer, more intense. It felt surprisingly good.

Paul drew back just enough to shower Dahlia with a lopsided smile. "Hey, as far as being beverage director of this party, I think I'm now permanently off duty," he whispered. "Let's make like a pair of bananas and split."

Nick's fingers flirted with the bare curves of Julie's body, his hands soft and warm under her shirt. She slid her hands along his lean, smooth torso, stopping at the waistband of his jeans. He stroked her back, kissing the small of her neck. Only a speck of guilt kept her from being overwhelmed, one tiny, misplaced stitch in a cloak of heady pleasure. She breathed in his scent, following his body with her hands. She felt a tremor of excitement go through her at the strange contours, the different way they fit together. She'd never held another boy so close, explored another body this way.

Nick kissed her mouth, a hard, passionate, searching kiss. Then a softer one. Julie heard him sigh, felt the soft exhalation as his lips released hers. She opened her eyes, and he was looking into hers. He shook his head, a faint, sad movement. "Time out. This is wrong," he whispered.

"I know." She held his gaze for a frozen moment. They kissed again. She drank in the salty moistness of his lips. It was wrong, but it was so sweet.

"Julie," he said. "We should stop, shouldn't we?"

Julie nodded, still holding him.

Nick let go of her. He let out a noisy breath. "Why do I always fall for girls who are going out with friends of mine?" There was a moment of silence. "Going out with? What am I saying? Married! To my friend. Julie, I love both you guys."

You guys. Her and Matt. At the mention of him, the stitch of guilt grew bigger. It stretched between them. "It's my fault," Julie admitted. She took a deep breath. "I should have known not to come over here in the first place. I think —well, maybe I was hoping this would happen. . . ." She wanted so badly to feel him hold her again, but she held back.

Nick gave a wry smile. "Hoping, but not hoping."

"Yeah, something like that," Julie confessed. "I mean it's like, I wanted it to happen, but outside my real life, you know? Outside the part of me that's married to Matt." Matt. One syllable spoken out loud and Julie knew it was over between her and Nick. Over before it had started. She shifted away from him.

"Julie, I guess it's pretty obvious how I feel about you," Nick said, "but I wouldn't want to purposely do anything to hurt the two of you. Really."

Julie nodded. "I like you, too, Nick." She touched his hand lightly. "Maybe a little too much. But—"

"But Matt's a pretty great guy," Nick finished for her.

Julie remembered how awful she'd felt as Matt took off on his motorcycle, how much she'd wanted him to come back, even though she was furious at him. "I wanted to work things out with him, make things better, not worse."

Nick nodded. "Then do it," he said. "I know Matt didn't come out here to let things between you fall apart."

Julie studied Nick's face—the fine, even features and square jaw, the blond-tipped eyebrows and intelligent eyes. The mouth she'd been kissing only a moment ago. At another time maybe she and Nick would have been together. "I guess I should go," she said quietly.

"I guess. I wish you didn't have to," he said.

Julie stood up, tucked in her shirt, then took

her coat from his desk chair. Part of her wished Nick would jump up and wind his arms back around her. She put the coat on, feeling him watch her as she fastened the log-shaped buttons.

She looked over at him. "Bye, Nick."

He gave an awkward smile. "Bye, Julie."

Twenty

❧

Three o'clock in the morning, and Matt still wasn't home. Julie had looked at the clock on the kitchen wall about a million times. She'd looked out the window nearly as often and felt herself jump at even the slightest sound of an engine in the distance, hoping, praying that it would be Matt's motorcycle.

Forget sleep. She sat in the living room armchair with her book open on her lap, but she wasn't even trying to read. *Don't get up again,* she told herself. *You just looked outside two minutes ago, and there wasn't a soul out there.* She shot a hard look at the telephone, not sure whether to will it to ring or not. What she wouldn't give to hear Matt's voice right now, his familiar, rough-grained tenor saying, "I'm fine, Jules. I'm on my way home."

But what if he wasn't fine? What if the phone rang and it was some stranger, calling with the worst possible news? Every nerve in Julie's body tensed. Matt had been in such a dark mood, and sometime during this interminable wait, it had begun to snow. To make matters worse, he still hadn't gotten around to replacing the brakes on his bike.

Julie tried to fight off the gruesome fear of an accident, but she knew all too well how easily it could happen. The night of Mary Beth's death would always be etched in her mind with horror and grief—one phone call, a race out to the site of the accident, and she'd never see her sister again. Julie didn't think she could ever live through that again. *Be okay, Matt. Please be okay.*

But her silent pleas were mixed with guilt. Was she somehow getting what she deserved? Waiting for Matt, longing for Matt, but with Nick's kisses still fresh on her lips. If Nick hadn't stopped when he did, would she have kept going? Even now, her heart beat a little faster at the memory of Nick's embrace, and she could feel her cheeks growing warm. For an absurd moment, Julie wondered if Matt knew what she'd done, and this was the result.

No. Of course not. It was just her shameful conscience.

Then why wouldn't Matt come home? Had he left her? Without a word? She fought the feeling of panic that grew with every sweep of the second hand on the clock. *Let him walk in that door,* she willed. *If he does, I'll never, ever again do anything like what I did tonight,* she promised herself.

Matt. The one who knew her deepest feelings, who could tell what she was thinking without even asking. Matt. The dark eyebrows over his deep-set gray eyes, the freckle near the side of his full mouth, the cute, squinched-up expression he had when he rolled out of bed in the morning, still half asleep. Suddenly it seemed so easy for Julie to remember why she loved him. She thought about how excited he got when he talked about music and the latest bands he'd heard, how much fun they had dancing together, how they'd stayed up talking until sunrise a few days before she'd left for school. She remembered the hot July evening when they'd climbed over the fence around the reservoir and gone swimming under the stars, and the day they'd hiked to the top of the highest peak in Pennsylvania.

The memories that felt so vague and thin

around the edges during the past few weeks were suddenly sharp and bright. *Don't let me lose him,* Julie prayed. *Let him come home. Please let him come home.*

She got up and began pacing the small living room. Her heart was beating too quickly, and she couldn't sit still. She found herself wishing, for one brief, unrealistic moment, that she could call home and hear her mother's reassuring voice, telling her everything would be all right. But there was no way she could call. Her parents would only say, "We told you so. We knew it couldn't work."

Julie positioned herself by the window to wait.

Dahlia felt a burst of daylight creeping into her dream. *Morning already?* Eyes closed, she pulled the blanket over her head, cherishing the dark warmth under the covers.

But just as she started falling back to sleep, a low drone, on and off, on and off, sounded in her ear. Dahlia pulled the cover down and opened her eyes. Paul Chase lay next to her, snoring his way through a deep sleep.

Ooops. The events of the night before flashed through her mind. The party. Nick and Julie leaving together. That gross guy Jeff X.

Oh, my God—had she really slept with a guy she'd known since kindergarten?

Dahlia sighed. Paul Chase. The guy she'd punched in the stomach in first grade. The guy who refused to talk to her from second through fourth grades. The guy who gave her the answers to math and science tests all through high school. The guy who'd been in love with her as far back as she could remember. The guy she'd gone to bed with just a few hours ago. Dahlia was wide awake now.

She looked over at Paul. He had the same crooked smile on his face in sleep as he had when he was awake. The pillow pressed his mop of curls against his face. No question about it, he looked funny.

Dahlia blushed as she remembered their lovemaking. It had been incredibly sweet and tender. Comfortable and comforting. But even while it was happening, she'd known it was the first and last time. *I shouldn't be here,* she thought, barely breathing, for fear she'd wake up Paul. She'd never wanted him to be anything but a friend. She knew it now, and she'd known it last night, too.

Why had she let it go so far? If she hadn't seen her best friend—her married best friend—leaving the party the night before with the guy she really wanted, she wouldn't have had to console herself in Paul's arms. Paul was a good friend, but Dahlia knew he wasn't Mr. Right. Poor Paul. How was she going to break the news to him? Gently, that's how, just as a friend should.

"Cool. Cool," Paul muttered in his sleep. He reached his hand out from under the covers searching for something. Dahlia put a pillow in his arms. "Cool," he repeated, smiling.

Same old Paul. Awake or asleep, Dahlia thought. She watched him turn over onto his stomach and bury his head under the pillow.

Should she tell him the truth now, right away, before he got it in his head that she wanted to be his girlfriend? *Good morning, Paul. I don't love you like you think I do.* On second thought, maybe it wouldn't be such a good idea to wake him up and give him such a harsh dose of reality that early in the morning.

Dahlia sighed. Somehow she always managed to dig herself into deeper and deeper trouble. She thought about all the rumors that had gone around about how she took advantage of people. Once again, she'd done it. But she hadn't meant to. Her night with Paul had been an accident. She wasn't any more guilty than he was, was she? Dahlia could only hope that Paul wouldn't take it too hard. They'd had enough problems already this year. She couldn't stand the idea of losing his friendship for good.

As gingerly as she could, she crawled out of bed. She was on the inside, against the wall, so she had to climb over Paul to get off the bed. He made a little grumbling sound but kept his head buried under the pillow and remained sleeping.

Dahlia slipped on her dress, gathered up her shoes and tights, grabbed her coat, and headed for the door. She turned and gave Paul a silent glance. *Please don't hate me too much,* she thought as she let herself out.

Julie banged on the door to her old room, her heart beating wildly. *Come on, Dahlia! Where are you?* It was seven in the morning. Dahlia should have been in there, fast asleep. Julie knocked again. "Dahlia, it's me," she said out loud, a frantic edge to her voice. But there was no answer, not even a sleepy groan or the rustling of sheets.

Julie slumped down in the hall in front of the door and put her head in her hands. She was so keyed up, she couldn't think straight. She'd done everything from listening to the radio for a report of an accident, to calling Matt's house

243

in Philadelphia and hanging up on his father's answering machine. She'd even dialed her parents, only to hang up before their phone started ringing. Trying to go to sleep while Matt was missing was totally impossible.

"Julie?"

She whipped her head up and saw Dahlia coming down the hall, her black coat flecked with sparkly drops of melted snow. She jumped to her feet. "Dahlia! Where have you been?" she asked, without waiting for an answer. "Matt's gone and I don't know what's going on, but he never came home and I think he's left me, or something awful's happened to him." Her words tumbled out one on top of the other. "I can't sleep. I've been up all night. I don't know what to do."

Dahlia walked toward her, a strange, tight look on her face. "What happened?" She put a hand on her hip. "Did Matt find out about you and Nick?"

Julie felt a jolt of shock. "Nick?" Suddenly her guilt-tinged fear became a reality. If Dahlia knew, then maybe Matt did, too, and that was why he'd left.

Dahlia took her key out of her pocket and jammed it in the lock. "Don't deny it, Julie." Her words were colored with anger. "I saw you with your arms around each other, and I know you left the party together."

Julie reeled under this new information. "That was because I'd just had a really bad fight with Matt. Dahlia, Nick was just trying to make me feel better." She followed Dahlia into the room.

"I'm sure he did just that, too," she snapped.

"It's not what you're thinking," Julie protested.

Dahlia spun around and looked Julie in the eye. "Julie, I've been hearing you talk about 'your friend' Nick since the beginning of the semester. It's pretty obvious how you really feel about the guy. And all Nick ever talks about is you. You don't really expect me to believe nothing happened, do you?"

Julie thought of the softness of Nick's lips and the way his body felt against hers. She knew her cheeks were burning. Guilty as charged.

"I knew it!" Dahlia took her coat off and threw it on the floor.

"Dahlia, it's not what you're imagining," Julie said.

"Julie, give me a break!"

"I'm serious." Why was Dahlia so angry, anyway? "It's not like Nick and I slept together."

Dahlia flopped onto her bed. "Come on, Julie. So what did you do? Study for a final or something? Right!"

"Dahlia, why are you yelling at me? Something terrible may have happened to Matt, and you don't even care!"

"Do you?" Dahlia challenged. "Look, Julie, even if you didn't sleep with Nick, it's pretty obvious you want to. I don't even know why you bothered to try to set Nick and me up. You're the one who really wants him!"

"Can't you forget Nick for a minute?" Julie's own voice was rising. "I'm talking about Matt. Besides, what difference does it make to *you* if I left the party with Nick?"

Dahlia was silent. Suddenly it was crystal clear to Julie what this was all about. "Oh, Dahlia, why didn't you tell me? I thought after that awful ride home over Thanksgiving that there was no way—"

"There isn't." Dahlia's anger was deflating into hurt. "I mean, the only reason the guy has anything to do with me is because I'm your friend."

"But you *do* like him," Julie said. She pulled out Dahlia's desk chair and sat down. "Why didn't you just tell me?"

Dahlia frowned. "Cozy, huh? We both like

246

the same guy. And he likes you. Except that you're married to someone else. *Married,* Julie. As in forsaking all others." Her voice was bitter.

"Dahlia, I know it," Julie said miserably. "And I'll admit I did get kind of turned around by Nick, but I think maybe it was more because of all the fighting with Matt. It was like, somewhere in the back of my mind, I thought it was easier to just start over with someone else. You know? I was running away from Matt because it hurt too much."

"And so you ran to Nick, and Matt split on you," Dahlia said.

Julie shook her head. "That's not the way it happened. I went over to the Barn and Grill to try and work things out, but Matt was so riled up he wouldn't even listen to me. He just rode away on his bike." She swallowed hard. "When I got back from the party, he still wasn't home."

"Oh," Dahlia said, rolling onto her back and staring up at the ceiling.

"Dahlia, don't be mad. Please," Julie begged. "I didn't know how you felt about Nick, and besides, I realized tonight that I don't want to be without Matt. Even if we're fighting. When I was standing by the window thinking that he might never come home—" Her voice cracked, and she couldn't finish the sentence. A tear

247

rolled down her face. "He's my husband," she whispered. "I love him. I want to be with him."

Dahlia let out a sigh, and her face softened. "He'll come home, Julie," she relented. "He probably just needed some time to chill out. It's understandable after everything that's been going on."

"But the brakes are all worn down on his bike," Julie said.

"Hey, if something had happened, you would have heard," Dahlia said. "Bad news travels fast. No news is good news."

"I guess." Julie and Dahlia sat in silence for a few moments. Julie felt at least mildly comforted by Dahlia's words. "Hey, thanks," she finally said. "And listen. About Nick? It didn't go very far. Really."

"Oh," Dahlia said, with a touch of envy on her face. "So—how does he kiss?"

Julie blushed. "Nice. But I wish I hadn't done it," she said quickly. "Dahlia, I just want to be with Matt and tell him how much I love him, in spite of everything that's happened lately. Nick's great, but what went on last night was a mistake. When I said for better or for worse, I meant it. I just hope Matt comes home so I can tell him that."

Dahlia gave a wry laugh.

"What?" Julie asked. She couldn't imagine what there was to be laughing about.

"Okay, so you goofed. Well, I guess I sort of goofed tonight, too. I have to admit something to you. I just slept with a guy who's practically my brother."

It took Julie a moment to realize what Dahlia was telling her. "Oh, no, Dahlia. Not Paul?"

Dahlia nodded. "Me and Paul."

"So that's where you were all night."

Dahlia propped herself up on one elbow. "I guess I got pretty bummed when I saw you and Nick leaving that party. Anyway, as usual, Paul was there to pick up the pieces. He was totally sweet, and one thing led to another. . . . I feel like such a jerk. I mean, the guy's my friend. I really care about him. But not that way."

"I know how you feel," Julie said. "Did you tell him?"

"Not yet. I left before he woke up. The major wimp-out."

Julie gave a dry, unhappy laugh. *Paul loves Dahlia. Dahlia loves Nick. Nick loves Julie. Julie loves Matt, who doesn't want to have anything to do with any of them.* "Big college kids, and all we can do is make a mess of things," she said.

Dahlia nodded. "You can say that again."

Twenty-one

✺

Matt pulled his bike up to the tiny cabin at the edge of the lake and shut off the engine. Riverville, Maryland. The town where he and Julie had gotten married. Here he was, right in front of their honeymoon cabin nestled between the water and the woods.

He sighed deeply as he got off his bike. A few months ago, this had seemed like the most romantic spot in the world. Now the porch of the cabin was hidden by a thin crust of snow, and the lake was a frozen blue, as if reflecting Matt's somber mood.

He thought back to the wedding day when he'd held Julie in his arms, his heart beating a pulse of bliss. They'd both felt it, certain that nothing could come between their love. Nothing.

Matt walked over to the edge of the lake, his boots crunching on the frozen ground. He took a few steps onto the ice. He couldn't help thinking that he and Julie had made a big mistake getting married so hastily. What was the big rush, anyway?

The truth was, except for Julie, he felt very much alone. Back in Philadelphia, he had lots of good friends. Here, there was only Julie. Sure, Nick and Leon were his pals, too, but Nick was usually busy with school, and Leon was always hiding away someplace playing his saxophone. And as far as work went, there was no comparison. Being manager of the Fast Lane had been the perfect job. Like throwing a party every night, only there was hired help to clean up. Here, he *was* the hired help. No matter how nice Jake and Pat were, being a glorified bus-boy couldn't hold a candle to his job at the Fast Lane—especially with all the bad feelings going around at the Barn and Grill recently.

If Matt had stayed in Philadelphia, he knew he'd be riding around on a brand-new motorcy-cle. Instead, that money had been spent on furnishing Julie's and his tiny apartment and paying rent. Just thinking about having to shell out most of his paycheck to cover next month's bills was horrible.

Matt ran a few halfhearted strides and slid along a patch of smooth, slippery ice trying to get up some winter spirit. But fun wasn't on the menu this morning. The wind blew a cold gust in his face. Matt let out a hefty cough. His body ached. A shiver ran the length of his spine. Now, on top of everything else, he was getting sick.

Julie. He'd done it all for her. But wouldn't she have been better off if he'd never come out to Madison in the first place? She wouldn't have always been so torn between him and college, dorm parties and nights home with her husband. What would have been so terrible about remaining boyfriend and girlfriend for a few years? Being temporarily separated for a while was supposed to have been a test for their relationship, to see if they would endure the time and distance. But they'd given up on that one right away. Given up and gotten married, without even thinking about what would come of it.

And now, in just a few short months, they'd lost the excitement of the present and the hopeful anticipation of sharing a forever with each other. Love and friendship, trust and understanding—Matt was realizing that even the most solid things could be shaken by the harsh reality of a day-to-day life together, the strain of making ends meet, the exhaustion at the end of a long day, the differences, small and large, in the way any two people thought and dreamed.

So what was keeping him from getting back on his bike and going the rest of the way to Philadelphia? He could be back in time to check in at the Fast Lane tonight. His father would welcome him with open arms.

So why didn't he hop on his bike and ride the rest of the way home? Home. That was the problem. Matt wasn't sure which way home was. He still loved Julie.

"You'd leave Julie, just like that? But she's the best and you know it!" Leon's words from the other day weighed heavy.

Matt had stopped at their honeymoon spot hoping to clear things up for himself. But just because he loved her didn't mean they'd made the right decision. Now Matt stood at the edge of a frozen lake, not sure which way he should go.

Fred held Marion's hands in his, rubbing them quickly. "Got to keep the circulation going. How's that?" Fred asked between chattering teeth.

"Better. Brrr. But I'm still freezing," Marion said, shivering.

"Just keep moving," he said.

All night long, they'd tried everything. Hugging, kissing, blowing warm air on each other's hands. They'd tried jogging around the sculptures. They'd even tried hugging and jumping up and down together as fast as they could. Anything for a little bit of warmth. They'd shared a few laughs and lots of kisses, but they'd shivered through the night.

Marion couldn't remember ever being so cold—even back on the farm in the middle of February when she milked the cows before school.

"Look!" Fred shouted. A smile spread across his face as he pointed to the rising sun, just barely visible over the tall hedges. "Warmth is here at last!"

But the bright orange ball looked, and felt, as if it was still ninety-two million miles away. "Brrr. Hurry up, sun," Marion prayed. "Do your thing."

Fred unzipped his coat and wrapped it around her. "Here, Marion, I don't need it anymore. The sun's enough to keep me warm. Mind over matter. I swear, I'm as warm as if I were on the beach in southern California."

"Then how come your teeth are still chattering?" Marion pulled him close and rubbed her arms up and down along his flannel shirt. "Better?"

"Brrr. I'm so warm!" Fred joked, hugging Marion tightly.

Suddenly Marion heard the sound of squeaky metal, like wheels rolling along a hard floor. "Fred. Listen! Did you hear that?" There it was again. The squeakiest, most wonderful sound in the world. "We're saved!"

Marion grabbed Fred's hand, and they raced to the door of the museum and started shaking the wrought-iron bars. "Hello! Help! Hello!" She looked inside and, sure enough, saw a figure approaching. "I think he hears us!"

A custodian was pushing a mop and bucket on wheels with one hand and holding a Styrofoam cup in the other. Marion could see him looking around to gauge where the noise was coming from. "Over here!" she shouted.

He started toward them. Closer. Closer. Through the glass doors and the iron bars, he stared at them, surprise in his eyes. She and Fred waved at him. He pulled the glass door open. "What the heck?!"

"We got locked in. I mean locked out," Marion said.

"We've been here all night," Fred added.

The man arched an eyebrow. Marion realized she was holding on to Fred in a real boy-friend-girlfriend sort of way. Did he think they'd done it on purpose, so they could be alone, just the two of them? "We were visiting the sculpture garden last night. And they must have locked up without even checking," she said. "We've been waiting for help all night, but—"

"Jeez, you kids must be freezing," he said, his voice suddenly filled with concern.

Marion and Fred nodded. "Can you let us out?"

"Sure. Oh, no, I don't have the key to the gate. It's Security." He scratched his head. "Tell you what. I'll go give 'em a call. Don't worry, kids, we'll have you out in a sec. Oh, hey, here, why don't you have my coffee? Piping hot. It'll help." He handed the cup to them through the bars of the gate.

"Thanks," Marion and Fred said. They both kept a hand on the cup. The moist heat felt wonderful on Marion's palms.

"You first," Fred said, pushing the cup toward her.

Marion took a sip of the coffee. "Finally, warmth." She could feel the hot liquid working its way through her whole body. She tipped the cup toward Fred's lips. He took a big gulp.

"Hey, will you have breakfast with me?" Fred asked.

"Definitely. But I'll meet you after I take about an hour-long steaming shower."

"Good idea." Fred leaned over and gave Marion a kiss on the cheek. Then one on the forehead, and then Marion brought her lips to his.

"Mmmm. I like how you kiss, Fred." Marion sighed with joy. She'd had the coldest night of her life, but now that it was over, it had been the most memorable, too.

Julie ran across campus, worry driving her every step. Was Matt lying hurt and alone on some icy back road somewhere, or in a hospital bed? Or had he really left her, giving up on their vows and their dreams? Or please, please —a silent chant accompanied her footsteps— was Matt back waiting for her, in their apartment, the home that they shared?

Julie was almost afraid to look and see if his motorcycle was parked at the curb in front of Secondhand Rose. But she sprinted the last few yards across the Green, making a sweep of Main Street with her gaze. She felt her heart flutter. Matt's motorcycle was there. He was home! He was safe! She slowed down just long enough to pat the shiny, blue gas tank of the bike before letting herself in the downstairs door and bounding up the steps two at a time.

"Matt? Sweetheart?" she called. Eagerly, she followed a trail to the bedroom: Matt's leather jacket dumped on the couch, his heavy boots near the entrance to the kitchen, and the rest of his clothes in a pile on the floor near the bed. As she came into the room, he turned his head on the pillow so he was facing her and opened one heavy-lidded eye.

"Hey," Julie said softly, tentatively. She stopped short of leaning over and kissing him, their fight still hanging between them like an invisible curtain.

But he gave a sleepy smile. "Hey," he echoed. In the weak, gray light that slanted into the room, he held a hand up toward her.

Julie felt her body go weak with relief. She took his hand and let him pull her toward him. She kissed his cheeks and his eyes and his nose. "I'm so glad you're home," she murmured.

"Me, too," he said, winding his arms around her.

They held each other in a tight hug. Julie drank in the feeling of his arms around her, the solid, comforting weight of his hands on her back.

"Let's never fight again. Ever," she said. She kissed the top of his head, inhaling him.

"Ever," Matt agreed.

She kissed his forehead. "Whoa! You're burning up!" she exclaimed.

Matt buried his face in the crook of her neck. "Yeah, I feel kind of awful. I think I just need a good night's sleep. In my own bed." Julie felt his breath against her skin. "I spent last night outside. Bet you can't guess where."

She hugged him even more tightly. "I spent the whole night worrying about that, Matt. I even called your dad's house and got his answering machine."

"Well, the truth is, Jules, I did start to go home. I mean back to Philly. But on the way I got kind of sidetracked." His words were punctuated by a raw cough. "See, I took a pit stop in this sweet town right over the Maryland border."

"You went to Riverville!" Julie had an immediate picture of the sweet, sunny little colonial town hall where they'd said their vows. It made her feel even happier to have Matt back.

"Yeah. I rode by where we got married—the brook's almost all frozen over. Then I headed out to the cabin and the lake." Matt turned onto his side so he was looking at her. "Jules, we said some real serious things to each other there."

"I know. And I meant them," Julie said. "Maybe I didn't realize how much until now."

Matt nodded. "Same." He took her hand and kissed her fingers. "So I guess it's not going to be a honeymoon all the time. So what?"

Julie laughed, the awful night she'd spent worrying already evaporating. That was one of the things she loved about Matt—the way he took things in stride. *So what.* So they were going to have to work harder to stay in love. It would just make the good moments feel even better. Julie's laugh turned into a yawn. "Mmm," she said, kicking off her shoes and climbing under the covers with Matt, without even taking off the rest of her clothes. "I could use some sleep, too."

She snuggled up to him and kissed him on the lips. He kissed her back. Softly, then more and more passionately. The kisses Julie knew so well. She ran her hands over the familiar lines of his body, the tight, flat stomach, the swell of his chest.

Uninvited, the fresh memory of Nick's lankier body surfaced in Julie's mind. She pulled back immediately. No. She didn't want those thoughts of Nick when she was holding Matt, caressing Matt. But she'd been in Nick's arms only hours before. She couldn't stop the comparison from barging into her thoughts.

"Hey, what's the matter?" Matt whispered. He tried to coax her closer again.

She resisted. Her guilt welled to overflowing. "Matt, I have to tell you something," she said. The tired, relaxed feeling was swallowed up in a new wave of nerves and regret.

"Can't it wait?" Matt murmured. He stroked her arm. "We have a lot of things we have to talk about—but later."

Julie shook her head. There was nothing she wanted to do more than put off her confession. But she knew she wouldn't feel comfortable in Matt's arms until she'd told him. "Don't hate me too much," she pleaded.

Matt's body tensed. Julie could see his guard go up. She took a deep breath, a huge gulp of air. "I kissed someone else last night."

A sting of hurt flashed in his eyes. There was a beat of silence. "Who?" he asked. The word felt like a punch.

Julie looked away from his pained gaze. "Don't be mad at him for it, Matt. It's my fault, not—not Nick's." Her voice dropped to a whisper as she said his name.

There was a stunned silence, then a blast of fury as Matt punched his fist into the headboard of their bed. "My friend Nick." He spat out his words bitterly. "How could you? How could he?"

"Matt, you have every reason to be angry," Julie said. She reached out and touched his arm. He pulled back as if she'd burned him. Julie felt a lump forming in her throat. "It was a mistake. I felt so terrible after you rode off, and he was trying to comfort me."

"He was certainly trying to do something," Matt said harshly. "I can't believe you. I really can't."

"We both knew it wasn't right. He feels as badly as I do."

"We. You and Nick. Cozy," Matt said, his fury heightened by disgust.

Julie blinked hard. "Matt, I love you. Don't think for a second that I don't." Matt didn't say anything. He flopped down onto his back. Julie watched him as he stared up at the ceiling, his jaw tight, his neck muscles tense. "Come on. I'm sorry. I wish it had never happened."

Matt gave an almost imperceptible shake of his head. "This stinks! I'm off in Riverville thinking about the day we got married—promised our love and devotion to each other—and you're here fooling around with one of the only guys I thought I could count as a friend."

"You *can* count him."

"Yeah, right."

"Matt? Remember in September when that thing happened between you and Traci?"

It took Matt a moment to answer. "We weren't married then."

"I know. And I remember how much it hurt me anyway. But it didn't mean you didn't love me."

"So then, if you love me, you can do anything you want, is that it?"

"No, it's not!" Julie's voice rose in frustration. "I went over the line. Way over—I know it. But it's not going to happen again, Matt. Ever. Trust me. Please."

"Oh, come on, Julie. You think it's that easy? Just mess up and expect me to say, 'Oh, it's okay honey, I understand. No big deal'?" Matt shook his head. "And what happens when you run into Nick around Madison? Hey, what happens when I do? Am I supposed to grin and act like nothing happened? At least you don't have to bump into Traci on the street every day."

"Nick is your friend."

"Then he should have kept his mitts off. Trying to steal you away from me is a pretty weird way to show friendship, don't you think, Julie? And going along with it is an even weirder way for you to show how much you love me." Matt rolled over and turned his back to her.

"Matt . . ."

"Look, Julie. I'm tired and I feel awful." He coughed, as if for emphasis. "I really don't know why I bothered coming back here. I want to go to sleep."

"I'm sorry, Matt. I really am." But Matt didn't respond. They lay next to each other without touching. Julie was afraid even to move. Every few minutes, Matt let out a harsh, dry cough. A little while later, she heard his labored breathing, slow with sleep but heavy with fever and illness.

She closed her own eyes. She was so tired. But sleep escaped her. She couldn't leave her misery behind even to dream.

Twenty-two

❧

Dahlia signed her name to the note and glanced over what she'd written. . . . *And whatever happened, I'm sorry if I led you on. I never meant to hurt you. I hope you'll forgive me.*

She sighed. She could only hope that Paul wouldn't bum out too much. She folded the note in half and looked for an envelope in her top desk drawer. Pretty wimpy, writing him a letter. But she just couldn't face telling him in person. It wasn't easy breaking up with a guy you'd known most of your life, especially when he'd been madly in love with you for most of those years. Dahlia couldn't stand the thought of seeing his crinkly smile go flat when she told him that last night had been a big mistake.

There was a knock at the door. A single rap, then a long pause, then three more knocks.

"Come on in," Dahlia called out. "Door's—Paul?!" she said, her face getting instantly warm. Well, she should have expected him to show up sooner or later.

"Hi," he said shyly. Only a trace of his crinkly smile was there, overpowered by the hesitation in his eyes. "Busy?"

"No, come on in. Have a seat, Paul," she said, nodding at the bed. *Ooops. I shouldn't have told him to sit there,* she thought. Once again, he'd get the wrong impression. Dahlia eyed the letter on the desk. Folded, thank goodness.

There was an uncomfortable moment of silence. Paul looked down at the floor. Dahlia was sure he was waiting for her to let him know where he stood. He wanted to hear that she'd fallen for him, that he was definitely the one and only.

Come on, let him down easy. The truth. Dahlia had to tell him now, live and in person. There was no other choice. "So—so what have you been up to all day?" she asked, stalling.

"Hanging out in the dorm. We had to clean up after the party. Some bonehead knocked over a full bowl of punch. I missed the worst part of the mess—woke up sort of late," he said, embarrassed.

"I'm sorry I left so early in the morning. It was pretty crowded in that single bed."

"It's okay," he said.

Long pause. Excruciatingly long. Then they both began speaking at the same time.

"Paul—"

"Dahlia—"

"Paul," Dahlia tried again. "About last night, I—"

"No, me first," he interrupted. "About last night. It's really hard for me to say this."

Dahlia felt herself start to panic. She couldn't bear to hear the words "I'm falling in love with you." "Don't say it, Paul," she pleaded.

"Dahlia, let a dude talk. This isn't easy," he said. "About last night. I—I'm sorry, but I think I made a mistake. I mean, I think we both did."

Dahlia's mouth dropped open. Had she heard correctly? "You mean—?"

"Look, I'm really sorry." He paused. "It's like this. You know how I've been the last few years. I've sort of been infatuated with you."

"Obsessed is more like it," Dahlia said, the words just coming out.

"Too true. You've been my dream girl for so long, Dahlia. And last night—wow!—my dream came true. Only, when it did, I guess I kind of realized it was a dream from my past. I mean, it's not like I didn't have fun and everything, but this morning the whole thing felt super weird to me. It's hard to explain, because I really like you and everything. But—"

"But you'd rather be my friend. My good friend, right?" Dahlia asked, seeing him nod as she finished his sentence for him. She felt a mix of surprise and relief—and a drop of injured pride.

"Right. I hope you don't, like, hate me or something. I'm sorry if I led you on. I didn't mean to. I guess I sort of didn't believe what was happening last night. I still don't, really. It's just that—"

"Paul," Dahlia said, grabbing the letter she'd written him. "Here." She handed it to him. "Read it and then tear it up, okay?"

Paul took the letter. Dahlia watched him read it. A smile spread over his face—the real, super-crinkly smile Dahlia knew and loved. He started laughing. "Why didn't you stop me earlier, Sussman? Before I poured my heart out."

"It sounded sweet." She smiled.

"And here I just spent the entire day wondering—whoa, how am I going to tell her?"

"What do you think I've been doing all day?" Dahlia laughed.

"Cosmic, huh? Hey, just for the record, I

broke up with you, right?" Paul finished reading the letter. "Really? You had fun? Me, too. That's half the problem, huh? We really did have our own party last night."

Dahlia smiled. "Cherish the moment, Chase. Now tear up the letter."

Matt lay in bed, his entire body racked with pain. While his head burned with fever, shivers raced through his body. One minute he was chilled to the bone, the next he was soaked with sweat. He strained to breathe. His lungs felt tight, and his throat was raw. It was next to impossible to swallow. He let out a deep, gravelly cough.

Julie had left a tray with juice and soup and a few motorcycle magazines on the table next to the bed. But Matt couldn't stomach the soup, and the juice only made his throat sting even more. He had tried to read, but his head pounded so badly he couldn't focus on the page. The television, too, made his head throb, so he just lay there, flat on his back.

Any degree of comfort was an impossibility. Eyes open, Matt felt nauseated. His head spun just looking at the corner where the ceiling met the wall. Closed eyes were even worse, conjuring up a jumble of confusing thoughts and images.

As if it weren't bad enough that he was sick as a dog, on top of that, he couldn't stop thinking about Nick and Julie. Together. Kissing. Was that all that had happened between them? How far had it really gone? Was it one kiss? Several kisses? As much as it hurt, Matt couldn't help but construct the ugly picture in his mind. There they were, Julie and Nick. Julie, the woman he loved. Julie, the woman he'd left home to be with. Julie, his wife, the woman who'd made a vow of trust to him. And Nick, Matt's closest male friend in town. Nick, the nice guy. Nick, who talked about how great Matt and Julie were together.

Running through his head was the rest of it, too. Everything. The fighting between him and Julie. The tension at the Barn and Grill. There was Carl making lewd comments about Julie. Sarah on the ground, screaming for help. Julie's article. The cops and all the hatred between the college kids and the locals.

In his head Matt heard his dad asking him to come back to work at the Fast Lane. He thought about Philadelphia versus Madison, about his overnight ride to Riverville. He remembered reciting his wedding vows. Matt couldn't come close to making any sense of it all. How had things gone so out of control?

And he couldn't shake the nagging feeling that maybe there was something else behind the problems—that maybe he and Julie *were* too young to be married, too unsure of themselves to have made the ultimate promise.

He heard footsteps coming up the stairs, then the door opening. "I'm home," Julie called out, her voice purposefully bright. "Matt?" She opened the bedroom door and smiled at him. "Hi."

Should he return the smile? She was trying so hard. She'd been taking care of him all day, leaving the house only for an early class, and to buy more juice, soup, aspirin, and cough medicine. "Feeling any better?" she asked.

Matt shrugged, his gaze wandering, refusing to meet hers. He could feel her hopeful eyes on him, but he just couldn't look up at her.

"You didn't touch the soup, Matt," she said, walking over toward him. "Come on, sweetie, you've got to try to eat a little. Here, I'll help you." She sat on the edge of the bed. "Matt?"

Finally, he picked his head up. Julie's large, brown, serious eyes were searching his for a sign of hope. Matt studied her, feeling himself holding back. Why had she strayed? Why had she broken their trust? Julie reached a tentative hand toward him, placing it on his forehead. "Wow, still burning up. I got some cold pills and some more cough syrup."

"Okay," he said, pulling away.

"Matt," she said softly. "I'm going in the other room and do some schoolwork. I'm there for you if you need me—if you want to talk or anything. But don't shut me out forever, okay?" She started to get up, but Matt reached out for her hand. Forever—it sounded too long.

"No, wait," he said. "Stay here, Jules." He let out a harsh, dry cough. "Jules, we have to talk. I can't keep this up any longer. I don't want to hate you. I love you. More than anything else. That's why I came out here. But if you're not happy with me, you've got to tell me now, so I can pack up and get on with my life."

"What are you saying?" Fright registered on her face. A tear trickled from the corner of her left eye. "You can't leave. I love you. Only you."

"Only me?" Matt frowned. "Then why—?"

Julie shrugged and lowered her head. "Because I'm human. I was confused—and I made a big mistake. I'll regret it for a long, long time." She looked back up at him, her eyes filled with regret. "Matt, you've got to believe

272

me. I got really mixed up. I'm sorry. I never meant to hurt you. Believe me, please?"

Why did she always sound so sensible? Matt did believe her. She had made a mistake and it *was* over. If only the picture would leave his head for good. "I just wish you hadn't—"

"I know, Matt. Me, too."

Matt let out a raw breath. "Listen, I know I had no right to split like that on you. Maybe I deserved what I got. I don't know. But I think it's about time we stopped hurting each other and started loving each other again."

"I like the sound of that. I'm willing to give it my best try." Julie smiled. Matt hadn't seen that wide-eyed, open face in a long time.

"Me, too. Hey, come here," he said, pulling her close. He wrapped his arms around her and felt the love, the real love. Julie buried her head in his chest. For a minute, Matt had an awful vision of Nick being there, too. But rather than let go, he hugged Julie even harder.

"I love you, Matt Collins. For better or worse, richer or poorer—"

"In sickness and in health, too, I hope." He let out another tremendous cough. "Let's not say the 'till death do us part' bit, because I feel like I'm about to croak." Matt felt her kisses against his feverish forehead.

"How about forever and ever," she said, her lips moving slowly along his face.

"Forever and ever," he murmured, as Julie's kisses followed his cheeks to his jaw and neck. Matt lay there, feeling the sweetness of her mouth on his face. His head still burned, and he was weak all over, but being loved felt like the best medicine on the market.

"Now just lie there and be a good patient," she said.

"Hey, you're not going anywhere, are you?" Matt asked.

"Who said anything about leaving? I just said to lie there and be a good patient. Now I've got you just where I want you—alone and in bed." She planted more soft kisses all over his face and forehead. Matt could feel some of the pain disappearing with each tender caress. Julie unbuttoned her dress and crawled under the covers.

"I'm going to get you sick," Matt said.

"I'll take my chances." He felt Julie's sensitive hands tracing a line from his chin to his chest. He returned her caress. Her skin was so soft, her scent intoxicating. His body tensed with pleasure.

Everything slipped away but the feel of her

lips, her warmth, her closeness. Her loose hair brushed his bare skin like a feather.

He pulled her closer, their bodies meshing, yearning to be one. As they made love, Matt felt the wonder and excitement of being with her. Her soul was there, in her caresses, meeting his. Their bodies, too, so warm and tender together, joined together until they were a single entity.

"Mmmm. Definitely worth a week in bed," Julie said as they lay happily in each other's arms afterward. "Maybe I'll get the flu right away, and we can spend the whole week together like this." She giggled.

"We've got some lost time to make up for, huh?"

She nodded. "And we've got forever, remember?"

"Oh, yeah. The two of us through eternity. You think we can stand it?" he kidded. "A college brain and a dumb townie together for a million years."

They both laughed for a minute. But then Julie took his hand in hers, her expression growing serious. "About all that, Matt. I'd like to make you a promise. That I'll never think anything less of a person just because he or she doesn't have a college education."

"And I'll never think anything less of someone because they *are* in college," Matt joked.

"Matt, I'm serious," she said.

"Me, too." He smiled. "From now on, equals, with or without, okay?"

"Deal," she said, shaking his hand. Matt held on and pulled Julie close for a kiss.

"I just wish the rest of this town could kiss and make up," she said. "You think things will ever be different here?"

Matt shrugged. "Let's face it, Jules, the town-gown thing has been around since day one, and it's not going anywhere."

"Sad but true, huh?"

Matt nodded. "Yeah, I don't think there's too much we can do. But I was thinking—while I was riding home from Riverville this morning —it's not all of them I have to try and change. It's me."

"But I love you the way you are," Julie protested, giving him a kiss on the forehead.

"You love me as a peon at the Barn and Grill?"

"It won't be forever, Matt," she assured him.

"No, it won't. And it's going to happen quicker if I do something about it," he said, sitting up. "And I already have an idea. A great idea, if I may say so."

276

Julie smiled. "I'm listening."

"It's called Club Night. Every Friday at the Barn and Grill. Live music up in the hayloft. I want to produce it, promote it, and—"

"Whoa, slow down," Julie said. "The hayloft at the Barn and Grill? How do you even get up there? I mean, it's all dark and gross up there, isn't it? What if the band and all their equipment fell through the floor?"

Between two hefty coughs, Matt managed a laugh. "They won't fall through. And it wouldn't be dark and gross if I cleaned it and put some lights up there, would it? I mean, Egypt was a desert, but they built the pyramids there anyway."

"Hey, I just remembered something," Julie said, starting to sound excited. "Last week at work, some of the women from town who work in the kitchen were complaining about having to drive an hour and a half last Saturday just to hear a decent live band. One of them was furious about not being able to drink beer because she had to drive home."

"See? It's got to work. I just have to convince Pat and Jake to go for it. I know it'll be good for their business, too. So you like the idea?"

"Uh-huh. I think it's great." Matt started to

get out of bed. "And where do you think you're going?" Julie asked.

"No time like the present. I've got to call them." But just as his feet hit the floor he felt a surge of dizziness. "Whoa. Spins."

Julie eased him right back down. "You stay where you are. I'll bring the phone in here." She stood up. "Club night? Yeah, it could work. My husband, the famous rock-and-roll promoter."

Twenty-three

❧

A Public Apology, Julie wrote. She leaned back in her chair in her little study carrel in the library and chewed at the end of her pencil. No, that wasn't what she wanted to say. She still stood by what she'd written about the attack on the Green. Now more than ever, she believed that women shouldn't be afraid to speak out. If Sarah had felt free to tell what had really happened to her, right at the beginning, there would have been far fewer bruised feelings in Madison, Ohio.

On the other hand, Julie had jumped to conclusions. She'd been guilty of not seeing past her own little college world. And she'd printed her opinion without thinking about the consequences. Speaking out was a responsibility, and you had to do it carefully.

She bent over her legal pad again and crossed out what she'd already written. *On Speaking Out,* she wrote instead.

"Hey, making yourself scarce?" said a voice at her back. Julie could feel her face turning red as she turned around. And Nick's familiar grin didn't quite cover up his own nervousness. For the past couple of days, Julie had been keeping her distance from Nick, purposely avoiding the spots where she was likely to run into him.

She didn't want to be reminded of their kisses, but now it was all she could think of with Nick standing so close, his green eyes studying her, his sandy-brown hair falling over his forehead. "Hi, Nick," she said guiltily.

"Hey," he said softly. "What're you working on?"

"Another newspaper article. Kind of in reaction to everything that happened after the last one," Julie said, looking past Nick to the metal bookshelves on the wall behind him. She felt too uncomfortable to meet his gaze. "I also want to invite everyone—town and college both —to Club Night."

"Club Night?"

"Yeah. See, Matt had this idea," Julie said. She told Nick what Matt was planning. "Jake and Patricia loved it. The first one is two weeks from Friday."

"Cool!" Nick said. "We could use something like that around here."

Then a silence stretched between them. "Um, you're going to be there, right?" Julie said. She tried to sound relaxed, normal, as if she were just talking to an old friend, but her voice came out higher than usual, a kind of forced casualness.

"I'll be there." Nick stuffed his hands in the pockets of his faded jeans and shuffled around uncomfortably. "So . . . it sounds like you and Matt are getting along better."

Julie couldn't hold back her smile.

"I'm glad," Nick said. "Really."

"Thanks. Me, too," Julie said.

The silence of the library enveloped them again. Nick cleared his throat. "Listen, Julie, about the other night," he said. "I'm really sorry. I should've had more self-control. A lot more."

Julie nodded and blushed. "Same here."

Nick took one hand out of his pocket and it hovered, like a bird without direction. It finally settled on the back of the chair at the next carrel over. "Um, is it okay if I sit down?" he asked.

"Oh, yeah. Sure. I should have asked you to." Julie was flustered. She'd always felt so comfortable with Nick. It was one of the reasons she'd grown attracted to him in the first place. And now they were both at a loss for how to behave.

Nick sat down backward, resting his arms on the back of the chair. "Julie, your friendship means a lot to me," he said. "I feel like I really messed up. If there's some way to fix things . . ."

"I hope we can," she said. But she knew, too, how hard it was going to be to get back to that easy feeling they'd had in the past. She took a long breath. "Um, Nick, I think I ought to tell you that I told Matt what happened between us."

Nick bit his lip and nodded slowly. "I figured you might." He was silent for a moment. "He hates me, huh?" he added unhappily. "I'm such a jerk."

Julie frowned. Not only had she made problems for her and Nick, she'd messed things up between Matt and Nick, too. Big time. "He's pretty mad," she admitted.

Nick let out a loud breath. "It's like what happened with Ben all over again."

"Allison's old boyfriend," Julie said.

Nick nodded. "Allison's boyfriend and my best friend. Ex–best friend, now." His face was grim. "I don't know what my problem is. Matt and I were really good buddies, and . . ." His sentence trailed off. "You think there's anything I can do?"

Julie shrugged. "Look, Matt doesn't have many friends around here. I know your friendship means a lot to him."

"Meant a lot," Nick amended. "I don't blame him if he never wants to talk to me again."

"Maybe it'll just take some time," Julie said. "You know, until everyone's temperature goes down." She wasn't sure if she believed her own words.

"I hope," Nick said. "Well, I guess I should let you get back to work." He stood up.

Julie looked up at him, feeling awkward. Their evening of intimacy now hung between them like a thick curtain. "Okay. See ya?"

"See you," Nick agreed. He turned and walked silently across the beige-carpeted library floor.

Julie watched his back as he went. The long, lean torso she'd caressed with her hands, the arms that had held her, the wavy, light-brown

283

hair she'd run her fingers through. And now they were even more nervous with each other than two people who had just met for the first time. She wondered if she'd lost his friendship for good.

Twenty-four

꙰

"Hey, I remember that dress!" Julie sat on Dahlia's bed and watched her take a slinky silver shift out of her closet. Dahlia had bought it at Secondhand Rose the first day they'd ever met. Now Dahlia held the dress up in front of her and turned to Julie for approval.

"What do you think? Can I wear it to Club Night, or is it too much?"

Julie laughed. "That's exactly what you asked me before you bought it, you know that? You asked me if it was too much to wear a silver dress in the middle of Ohio. I thought you were so daring. In fact, I was pretty much in awe of you."

Dahlia draped the dress over her desk chair and started removing her jeans and T-shirt. *"You,* in awe of *me?* No way. You were the one who was all smart and together. Serious boyfriend, perfect family. I figured you'd think I was a total flake."

"Yeah, well, I wish my family was a little more perfect these days," Julie said as Dahlia pulled the silver dress over her head. It glinted and gleamed as she wriggled into it. "But the Matt part, well, since we made up it's been really nice." She smiled, thinking about how she'd opened her eyes this morning and found Matt propped up on one elbow, watching her, in the weak winter light.

Dahlia rummaged around in her top drawer. "Sounds like you guys are in married bliss these days."

"Mmm. Pretty much. Except that Matt's been kind of sick. He's nonstop coughing. He's still got the flu or something." She watched Dahlia pull a pair of shiny pearl-gray hose on over her long, shapely legs. "Wow! You look totally great! Look out, Madison, Ohio." Julie felt too covered up by comparison in her loose black silk trousers and dolman-sleeved sweater.

"Thanks." Dahlia peered into the mirror on her wall. "I feel kind of funny about going without a date. I mean, I never went out without one in high school. But, hey—maybe someone we know will be there and maybe sparks will fly."

Dahlia took her makeup bag from the top of her dresser. "Yeah. And maybe they won't. Who am I kidding, anyway?" She shook her head, her blond hair swirling around the silvery fabric of her dress. "Nick and I are still at the 'hi, how are you?' stage. I doubt we'll ever get any further than that."

Julie sighed. "Yeah, well, if it makes you feel any better, it's not so different with him and me these days. I mean, we're both trying, but it's still pretty uncomfortable. Especially since Matt's not even talking to him."

"Maybe Nick should come to Club Night in disguise," Dahlia said wryly. "The tall, handsome mystery man rides into town."

Julie laughed. "That's not the worst idea."

Dahlia jabbed the mascara wand into the tube. "Yeah, well, I have to wonder why I bother with the guy. I mean, I don't want to sound egotistical or anything, but there are plenty of other guys who'd like to go out with me. I can't figure out why I'm so stuck on wanting Nick."

"You just said it. Because you're so used to having anybody you want. But—"

"You mean since I can't have him, I want him even more? Yeah, that sort of makes sense, I guess." Dahlia applied her mascara and then closed the tube. "But I think there's more to it than that. I suppose it also has something to do with the fact that the guy's totally gorgeous." Dahlia raised her eyebrows in an exaggerated motion, and she and Julie both started laughing.

"But anyway, I'm going to have fun tonight no matter what," Dahlia said.

"Me, too." Club Night already seemed like a success. A huge smile stretched across Julie's face. It felt like a long time since she'd just let loose and had fun. She didn't think she could lose tonight. And neither could Matt.

The Barn and Grill was packed. Bathed in a wash of cool blue light punctuated by a flickering strobe, the electrifying pulse of Looney Tunes poured out from the hayloft above. Their unique blend of down-home pedal steel twang with explosive rock-and-roll riffs was perfect for the occasion. The band seemed to meet the needs of both sets of ears, college and town, alike. The two factions were still pretty much separated by the middle aisle, but with less of the tension of the past few weeks. Matt felt proud as he raced around from table to table, taking orders, serving burgers and beers, and making sure everyone was having fun. Club Night was an instant success.

He looked toward the front door and noticed another half-dozen people paying their admission. One of them was arguing with the bouncer. Matt figured the guy had slipped him a fake ID so he could get his hand stamped and be served alcohol. The bouncer shook his head no, and the kid threw his arms up in a huff. But Matt saw the scowl slip off his face as soon as he walked inside.

"Burgers!" Pat called out from the kitchen.

Matt wove his way through the packed room to the service window to get them. On the way he received a hefty pat on the back from a guy wearing a Madison College sweatshirt. "Great party, man. Great tunes! Thanks, dude." Matt recognized the guy from the night of the fight. He was sure he was the one whom he'd tried to yank off Carl. Jake and Pat were definitely right when they said they'd all come back as if nothing ever happened.

"The rare burgers are for Marcy's table," Pat yelled to Matt through the window. "The others are for tables six and seven, okay?"

"Got it." Matt reached for the tray from the counter. "And six more burgers, well done, and fries," he said. "Table eleven."

"Slow it down, will you?" Pat wore her usual overworked but happy face. She wiped her forehead with a damp cloth and put it back in her apron pocket. "I think you got the whole state of Ohio in here."

"Just don't forget those burgers," Matt said as he started to go.

"Hey, Matt," Pat said. "Did Jake and I tell you we think you're a genius?"

"Yeah, but you can tell me again." He laughed. "I love hearing it."

"Okay, you're a genius. Seriously, Matt. Thanks. We've needed something like this for a long time. Look how happy everybody is out there. You really hit on something."

"So, you think we'll do it again?"

"How does next Friday sound? Are you going to have a band for us?"

Matt knew his elated smile told all. "Definitely." The wheels were turning. Crazy Fingers was coming to Cleveland next week. They might have time to do a show here. And Summer Southerland was coming to Ohio in February. Maybe she'd do a late-night set at the Barn and Grill. Club Night in the hayloft. The possibilities were endless. "I won't let you down," Matt promised, scooping up the tray and heading over to Marcy's table.

Matt handed her and her friends their burgers. "Here you go."

"Rare, I hope!" Marcy shouted over the music.

"See for yourself," Matt yelled back. If she was in one of her moods tonight, Matt wasn't playing.

"Perfect," she said. She cracked a little smile and handed him a bill. "Keep the change, honey."

Matt shook his head, laughing. He put the tip into an already filled apron pocket. He was well on his way to having a whopping night at work. Tips were rolling in. But even better, Matt knew that half the profits from the door were his, too. He'd made a fifty-fifty deal with Pat and Jake. After band expenses and the cost of the security guard, half of the take would be Matt's.

"Burgers!" Pat called out again. Matt finished delivering the plates on his tray and went back to the kitchen to collect another round.

"Listen, why don't you take five after you serve these, Matt?" Pat suggested. She gestured to a table near the front of the restaurant. Julie was sitting there with a group of friends from her old dorm.

"Hang with Julie for a bit," Pat said. "Go

ahead. I won't have any more food ready for at least ten minutes. Jake and I can handle it."

"Thanks, Pat. Hey, could you do me a favor?" Matt pointed to a table in the far corner. Nick was sitting with a couple of guys. "That table over there, they ordered three Cokes and a couple of medium burgers. Could you serve them? I'd rather not." Matt had taken their order, but he had barely been able to bring himself to say hello to Nick. It was still too painful. Nick had been somber and uncomfortable, too.

"Sure, Matt," Pat said.

"Thanks." Matt took the tray of burgers, leaving the two for Nick's table for Pat.

On his way over to Julie's table, he passed Leon, dancing up a storm with Dahlia. They looked totally cool together. Dahlia, center stage, was shaking it, her silver dress dazzling. Leon, in a thrift-store black tux, had stepped out in style, too. "This girl can dance!" he shouted as Matt went by.

Matt snuck up on Julie from behind. He put a hand on her shoulder and gave a little squeeze. "Hi, beautiful."

Matt heard her laugh before she turned around. "Yeah! My hero!" she said as she twisted around. She blew him a kiss. "I was going to order more food just so you could come to our table."

"Want to dance?"

"Really?" Julie's smile was so beautiful. Soft, round, rosy cheeks. Matt's favorite face in the world. He was ready to gather her up and hug her until they both melted away.

The fast beat of Looney Tunes didn't matter. Matt held Julie close, and they danced slowly, pressed tightly together. He gave her a gentle kiss on her bare neck. "Happy ending, huh?"

"Couldn't be better," Julie said. "It sort of feels like the Fast Lane in here. Everyone's having a blast. This is the best party of the decade."

"That's because I'm a genius," Matt joked, kissing her on the neck again, in the same, sweet-smelling place. "Have I ever told you how beautiful you are?"

"Uh-huh. Mmmm. Keep kissing me, Matt. It feels wonderful. I'm so happy."

"Me, too. And guess what? Pat and Jake are psyched for next week. Club Night's really going to happen!"

"Really?" Matt felt Julie's excited hug. "I'm so proud of you, Matt!"

"Yeah. Hey, I was thinking about how we'd spend the first million. I still owe you a real honeymoon. How about a trip around the world, no expenses spared. We could—" Julie's lips pressed against his. "Okay, maybe it would be smarter to figure out how to spend the first hundred. The million might take some time." She kissed his forehead.

"Hey, you're still burning up, Matt. You've been running yourself ragged every day for the past two weeks. You should be in bed," Julie said, placing a hand on the spot where she kissed him.

Her hand felt cool against his warm, sticky skin. As if at the power of suggestion, Matt was coughing again. He'd been so busy planning Club Night, he'd ignored the fact that he was still sick. "I'm just overworked," he assured Julie, trying to believe it himself. "I wouldn't have missed tonight for anything. Anyway, I've got Sunday and Monday off, so I'll get some rest then."

"Promise?"

"Don't worry, Jules, I'm fine." But the truth was, Matt was starting to get a little worried. His fever came and went, but he'd been coughing for nearly two weeks, and his throat still felt like sandpaper. Maybe it was time to see a doctor.

Matt caught sight of Pat putting an order of

burgers up on the ledge of the service window. "I guess I've got to get back to work, Jules."

"Too bad. But I'll be saving all my dances for you." She reached up to put her hand to his mouth. "I love you, Matt. More than ever."

"Don't say those things to a guy who's got to go to work." Even sick, he felt like the luckiest guy on the planet.

Don't miss **In Sickness and In Health,**
the next book in this dramatic series.

Matt glanced up toward the apartment window. He caught sight of Julie waiting there and waved, his mouth forming a little smile. But his smile looked unsteady.

Julie breathed in sharply. As Matt reached the downstairs entrance, she whirled away from the window and rushed to the door of their apartment. She felt queasy. She pulled open the door and raced down the stairs to meet him.

On the stairs, Julie threw her arms around him in a fierce hug. "Well?" she whispered.

"Well, how about letting me get inside and sit down, beautiful?" he said lightly. But his tone was too deliberate. Julie could feel him measuring out his words.

"Please, Matt," she implored. Matt was too controlled. If it were good news, he would have spilled it the second he saw her. She felt sick with fear as she followed him to the living room.

Her eyes were fixed on Matt as he took off his jacket, draped it over the arm of the sofa, and sat down. He held out his hand. She took it, letting him pull her down next to him. Matt squeezed her hand tightly as she settled into the cushion. He looked at her. Deep-set gaze. Serious gaze. Julie needed to know, but suddenly she wanted to stop his words.

"It's Hodgkin's Disease," he said quietly.

Julie's feelings were suspended on a current of shock. "Hodgkin's?" she heard herself repeat dully.

"Cancer," Matt said, without displaying any emotion himself.

THE SUN IS HOT...
AND SO ARE THE GUYS ON
FAR HAMPTON BEACH.

Especially Reed. Jess can't get him out of her mind.

Then his snobby girlfriend, Paula, shows up. Paula always gets what she wants.

But not this time... if Jess can help it.

DON'T MISS

Lifeguards

LG1192